D1020129

The Love She Left Behind

ALSO BY AMANDA COE

What They Do in the Dark

A Whore in the Kitchen

AMANDA COE

The Love She Left Behind

A NOVEL

W. W. NORTON & COMPANY
NEW YORK • LONDON

The Love She Left Behind is a work of fiction. All of the characters are products of the author's imagination, and all of the settings, locales, and events have been invented by the author or are used fictitiously. Any resemblance to actual events, or to real persons, living or dead, is entirely coincidental.

First American Edition 2015

First published in Great Britain under the title *Getting Colder*

Printed in the United States of America

For information about permission to reproduce selections from this book, write to Permissions, W. W. Norton & Company, Inc., 500 Fifth Avenue, New York, NY 10110

For information about special discounts for bulk purchases, please contact W. W. Norton Special Sales at specialsales@wwnorton.com or 800-233-4830

Manufacturing by Courier Westford
Book design by Brooke Koven
Production managers: Devon Zahn and Ruth Toda

Library of Congress Cataloging-in-Publication Data

Coe, Amanda, 1965–
The love she left behind : a novel / Amanda Coe. — First American edition.
pages cm
ISBN 978-0-393-24549-3 (hardcover)
1. Married people—Fiction. 2. Dysfunctional families—Fiction. I. Title.
PR6053.O25L68 2015
823'.914—dc23
2015004620

W. W. Norton & Company, Inc.
500 Fifth Avenue, New York, N.Y. 10110
www.wwnorton.com

W. W. Norton & Company Ltd.
Castle House, 75/76 Wells Street, London W1T 3QT

1 2 3 4 5 6 7 8 9 0

For Gus and Julia

The Love She Left Behind

What happens in the heart simply happens.

—TED HUGHES, *Birthday Letters*

I think the rage to understand comes from the fact that you do not ask the right question. You will never find the right answer if you do not ask the proper question. It's like trying to open a door with the wrong key.

—LOUISE BOURGEOIS

Part One

Now

SPRING

THERE WAS no one left to call him Nidge. This had been his first clear thought when Patrick's neighbour rang to tell him their mother was dead. Seeing Louise step off the train the morning of the funeral, Nigel realised it was also possible for her to call him Nidge, although she didn't tend to call him anything. The ability to use his childhood name was a small power Louise didn't know she could exercise, and the fact that she didn't added to his irritation at the sight of his sister's pilled coat and misjudged cleavage. Immediately worse than any of this, though, was the teenage girl that unexpectedly followed her out of the carriage door, helping to bump a wheeled bag down on to the platform. Swaddled in a puffa coat that enhanced her matronly bulk—a miniature version of her mother's—she was much changed since Nigel had last seen her, when she must have been around seven.

'I had to bring her,' said Louise. 'She's been poorly and I couldn't get anyone to look after her. I can't rely on our Jamie, can I, Hol?'

Nigel allowed the cough he'd been suppressing in his throat all morning full rein; the pollen count must be off the scale. Holly. Sophie would have remembered straight away; she took care of birthdays and Christmas. Not for the first time since he'd arrived in Cornwall, Nigel regretted his ready agreement that his wife would stay home with the boys while he navigated Mum's funeral solo. *Holly*. He nodded a hello and instructed himself to stop coughing; it was an itch always there to scratch, and once the membranes were inflamed, restraining himself became a torment. His niece sniffed back her own lacklustre greeting, fortunately too apathetic to share her germs. She was unappealingly pale and pink-eyed: presumably the result of her illness. Nigel supposed it would be fine for her to attend the ceremony. He couldn't imagine they'd exactly be oversubscribed at the crematorium. Still, it was aggravatingly like Louise to spring a surprise on him.

'It's a good job you let us know when everything's happening,' said Louise, as he led them out of the ticket hall to the parked funeral car. 'Have you seen him?'

'I've spoken to him on the phone. About the arrangements for today.'

This had been Nigel's plan, to pick Louise up from the station first so that they would face their stepfather together. Patrick had, of course, been too distraught following their mother's death to make any of the phone calls himself, even the first one. This had been left to a neighbour, Jenny, the kind of competent middle-aged woman presumed on as a brick. Patrick was all too ready to presume, but Nigel's legal training was an obvious qualification for him taking over all that was to follow, if being a son hadn't been sufficient in itself. It qualified him over Louise, anyway, unquestioningly. He had made the necessary calls following Jenny's initial contact, and all the subsequent arrangements. This landed on top of a busy time at work, but he made lists and forged through them, as always, despite an electric cable of sciatica that shot down his leg whenever he sat down. In the days following his mother's death, Nigel had made quite a few calls with acupuncture needles sticking out of him like the miniaturised afflictions of a medieval saint. Despite the osteopath's admonitions, it hadn't stopped them working, if it was in fact the needles that had erased the pain rather than the large doses of anti-inflammatories Nigel had been taking in secret defiance of the alternative remedies Sophie had arrayed on his bedside table. In any case, today only the hay fever was laying him low.

'So, we're picking Patrick up, the service is at eleven thirty, nothing fancy—then it's sandwiches and so on at a hotel back near theirs.'

'Lovely.'

Watching Louise fuss her daughter into her seatbelt, fumbling the prong blindly at the catch with an exclamation at each failure until Holly herself took the strap and housed it with one click, Nigel remembered acutely why he had no time for his sister. In the roughly three-year intervals at which they saw each other, nothing changed. Or rather, her circumstances changed—usually worsened—but Louise didn't. Soon she would start talking up a plan born of a low-level but persistent crisis: training, relocating, paying off a loan, finishing with her boyfriend, finding a different house, laying down the law with her kids, losing the weight. None of it ever happened.

'How long do you think they knew she was ill?' Louise asked, once their car had pulled away from the station. Of course, there were other things to talk about today: Mum. Deliciously, Nigel rolled his tongue up against his palate, which itched furiously.

'No idea.'

With Patrick out of bounds with grief, there had been no one to talk to except Jenny the neighbour. Nigel had scarcely felt he could assail her with questions about their mother's final months and days. The bare bones of it was undiagnosed stomach cancer—diagnosed so late that Mum had had scarcely a week before she died at home, hospital being pointless at the stage it had been discovered. Perhaps during the reception (the hotel had been recommended by the funeral home), Jenny might be able to tell them more. After a drink, which Nigel was already greatly looking forward to. With the amount of Sudafed he'd taken, it would hit him like a train.

'So, this is Cornwall!' Louise's tone was brightly officious, attempting to engage Holly, who was staring glumly through the view from the window. 'Fab, isn't it?'

Neither Louise nor her daughter had ever been to the house they were travelling to. Having Louise here, large and human behind him in the formal black car, Nigel felt to his marrow the strangeness of this accepted fact.

'They didn't even admit her to hospital, you know—it must have been very far gone,' he said.

'Did *she* know, though?' Louise shifted forward, filling the space. 'She must have, surely. You'd think Patrick would have let us know—let you know. So we could say goodbye.'

That was the way Louise liked to do things. A bedside goodbye, as in the soaps she watched. Tearful reconciliations. Not that reconciliation was necessary, as far as he knew.

'Mum, I feel sick.'

Surely the girl's voice, with its strong Yorkshire accent, was too small and childish for her age? Louise leaned across her daughter to work the window switch. It didn't respond. She bent forward to the driver.

'Do you mind if we have a bit of fresh air?'

The window retracted, blasting icy wind at the back of Nigel's neck and increasing his irritation. Louise insisted the window stay open for the entire route—along a winding B road—to counteract Holly's possible nausea. By the time they pulled into the potholed drive, Nigel could see in the rear-view mirror that Louise's thin hair had been whipped into a demented mop. She looked older than the last time he'd seen her, despite highlights and too much makeup. Worn, with cross-hatching beneath her eyes. His own eyes were streaming.

'You'll have to put the window up, for Patrick,' he told them both, getting out.

Phase two: Patrick. If Louise demanded patience, Patrick demanded a whole armoury of seldom called-upon resources. It would be like playing squash with a county champion after a ten-year layoff.

Walking up to the door, Nigel recognised a nest of broken, empty plant pots that had seemed temporary on his last visit, lichened into permanence. Although not as alienated as Louise from the Patrick/Mum axis, it was in fact at least ten years since Nigel had been to the house. It had scarcely been a show home then, but now the façade spoke of long-term neglect, its windowsills scabbed with grey, flaking paint and the grizzled creeper hanging over the front porch in an unpruned, brittle mat. Despite this, Nigel still enjoyed an atavistic buzz at the fairy-tale existence of such a large family asset. Patrick wouldn't be able to live here on his own, not without being able to drive. And even so unfashionably close to Newquay, it couldn't be worth less than half a million.

'You said half past.'

Patrick had opened the door before Nigel could knock. Unchanged in the dark hallway, when he stepped outside, daylight revealed him to be shockingly old and shabby. He was wearing that disgraceful raincoat he'd always had, the colour of something on a butcher's tray. Unbuttoned, it revealed a bobbled fleece mapped with food stains, worn over a shirt and tie. Both fleece and tie, at least, were black. And like the house, the quality of Patrick's architecture defied neglect. The nose still arched, the lip, if a little thinner, still curled. As they walked to the car, the wind blew Patrick's coat open and revealed a Norwich Union logo on the breast of the fleece. Presumably he had got it free.

'I've been waiting.'

'We had to pick up Louise.'

Patrick balked as though confronting a tripwire. Even he must have known that Louise was certain to come to Mum's funeral; she was her daughter. You couldn't even call her estranged, exactly. And there was certainly nothing Patrick could do about it now. Nigel strode round to the passenger door and held it open, like an employee. An explosive sneeze compromised his chauffeur's stance as Patrick made his shambling approach. He pulled up again.

'Who's this?'

The girl, Holly, was now sitting in the front seat, her hands pressed prayerfully between her thighs. Nigel saw Patrick's momentary confusion at a collapse of time where this child could be Louise, before Louise herself, fully and massively contemporary, clambered out of the back to explain.

'Holly. Patrick, it's me, Louise—this is Holly. My daughter. I'm so sorry.'

After a moment of paralysis, Louise lurched in to embrace Patrick. She curtailed her gesture into a brief clutch at his neck as he failed to respond, still unwilling to share anything of their mother with her, even her loss. He got in the car. Louise's eyes magnified with tears.

'She felt sick on the way; she hasn't been well. The driver said she'd be better off in the front.'

Phase three: the funeral. It was fifteen miles to the crematorium. With Holly in the front, the three of them were forced to sit together in the back. It was, as far as Nigel remembered, an unprecedented configuration. Despite the roominess of the estate car, he leaned defensively against his window. It was Louise who broke the silence, a few minutes on to the motorway.

'Have you had any breakfast, Patrick?'

Although Patrick was clearly stunned by the audacity of any question at all, its sheer simplicity compelled an answer.

'Um, no.'

'It's going to be a long day,' she said over his head, to Nigel. 'Maybe we should get something on the way—we've got time.'

'I don't want anything,' Patrick said.

'You'll be dropping,' Louise persisted. 'Even a cup of tea—have you had a cup of tea?'

Patrick shrugged an apathetic negative.

'We could stop at a garage,' said Louise. 'They'll have a machine.'

Nigel decided to knock this one on the head. Their slot at the crematorium started in less than half an hour. He had persuaded the bookings clerk to rearrange another family in order to get the uniquely convenient late-morning time, which would permit him to get home to Surrey that night. If they missed it, it would be like trying to find runway space at Heathrow.

'I don't think we've got time—'

'I need to get some fags,' said Patrick, exploring his coat pockets. So that was that. The driver pulled into a station pennanted with some unfamiliar local logo and Louise took Patrick's order for twenty Silk Cut Light.

'Can't smoke in the car, sir.' The driver instinctively addressed Nigel. He was, after all, the only one in a suit. Nigel checked his watch, resisting the temptation to rub his gritty eyes. At the funeral, he supposed, everyone would take their redness as a sign of grief.

'How long will it take us now?'

''Bout twenty minutes, give or take.'

They really didn't have time to wait for Patrick to smoke a cigarette. Louise took an age getting the bloody things as well, as they all waited in a silence broken only by a few harrowed sighs from Patrick. Finally she reappeared, her lengthy absence explained by the lidded disposable cup of tea she carried, along with a grab bag of crisps and a plastic bottle of Coke that she dangled over to Holly in the front.

'I thought she was ill,' Nigel objected.

'She hasn't had any breakfast.'

The girl waved away her mother's offerings.

'Can't eat in here, if you don't mind,' said the driver, gently.

'Oh well.' Louise stuffed the refreshments into her bag and asked Patrick what combination of the milk pots and sugar sachets pincered between her fingers he wanted in his tea.

Five minutes back along the road, Patrick crumpled the cellophane from the Silk Cut packet into the footwell of the car and took out a cigarette. Nigel made a move as he saw the driver clock this in the mirror.

'Patrick, you can't smoke in here.'

Arrested in trawling a disposable lighter up from a far corner of his raincoat's lining—the pocket must have been lost to a hole—Patrick halted and jabbed at the window button.

'It's all right—'

'No smoking if you don't mind, sir.'

'I can't open the bloody window!'

'He has to work it from the front—' Louise told him.

'You can't smoke in here—'

'What?'

Nigel pointed ahead to the neat sticker on the dashboard, with its universal symbol. 'You can't smoke in here, Patrick. It's a no-smoking car.'

Patrick's convulsion of contempt was vast, familiar, and still frightening. Louise just managed to save the tea.

'Christ alive—can you not open the window?'

'Sorry sir, it's company policy.'

'My wife's cold in the ground, man.' Patrick sparked up, inhaled. '*Company policy.* How about human fucking decency?'

The window rolled down to its limit.

'I'm a smoker myself, as it happens,' the driver said, nervously tracking the direction of the smoke. He was an older man, small, with yellowed whites to his eyes.

'Muuum.'

Louise shifted.

'I'm sorry, Patrick, cigarette smoke makes Holly feel sick.'

Patrick continued to smoke.

'She's been feeling sick.'

'I think I'm gonna *be* sick.'

'Oh you're not, are you, love?'

'I feel really sick.'

The girl's voice had risen an octave again, back into childishness. She did look very pale. The wind was whipping away most of Patrick's smoke.

'Patrick, please!'

'Tell her to try putting her head between her legs.'

Louise changed position. For a wild second Nigel thought she was going to attempt to grab the cigarette from Patrick and throw it away, but she was only stretching forward to get a better look at Holly.

'Are you going to be sick?'

The girl nodded violently.

'I'm sorry,' said Louise to the driver, 'we'll have to stop.'

'We're going to be late!' Nigel objected.

'It can't be helped, can it?' Louise rolled a look past Patrick to Nigel. Surprised, he caught it, just as an annihilating sneeze tore out of him. Why hadn't he listened to Sophie about getting her mum to babysit and let her come with him?

The driver pulled on to the hard shoulder. Louise massaged Holly's back as she bent over the rusted barrier at the verge, hair hanging in strings. Patrick finished his cigarette.

'Suppose they can hardly start without us,' Nigel reassured himself. Careless of the consequences, he raked his palate frantically against his tongue. Holly produced a couple of dry retches.

'Oh *Christ*.'

The spent butt pitched out of the window, Patrick swigged the last of his petrol-station tea. As his jaw stretched, Nigel saw that he'd missed a patch when he'd shaved, close to his ear. The stubble was silvery, both unspeakably louche and terribly vulnerable. Outside, Holly was holding her stomach, Louise still bent to her. Nothing happened.

Why did it always have to be like this? Why would it be any different? Mum was dead. It was the only thing that had changed. Sophie should have come with him, definitely, but it was better that she hadn't. Tenderly, Nigel placed a cool forefinger on each closed, raging eyelid. This worked, sometimes.

'Women,' said Patrick.

March 10, 1978
Cobham Gardens
Early hours.

Darling Dear Girl,

I'm sitting here drinking whisky and unable to write a word and thinking how very much I love you and want you and can't live without you.

I want to fuck you three times in a row.

This will never do, will it?

Patrick xx

HER MOTHER HAD had a way with clothes. Even in the chaos of the wardrobe and its overflow into the bedroom, Louise could see this hadn't deserted her. So far, she had come across no garments that she recognised, yet they were all familiar in expressing the singularity of her mother's style. Part of it, she could see now, was money; old clothes that didn't date or wear out. A good coat—that was something she could remember Mum harping on about. You need a good coat. It must have helped that she had stayed the same size for years, by the look of it, although she would have been emaciated by the end. Stomach cancer: how could it have been otherwise? Surely she must have known, long before that solitary collapse in the Tesco car park and the hurtling deterioration of her final week? Other, more secret parts of your body might harbour a tumour unknown to you, but surely not your stomach.

Louise hadn't asked for a look at Mum in the casket before they burned it. There was no point in seeing how much she had changed, except to upset herself. All the funeral rituals demanded you recognise death as real when it was the last thing you wanted, each impersonal stage stripping away what you held on to, finally trundling her away up a conveyor belt like a supermarket item to be scanned and bagged. And without them saying goodbye.

At least now there was all the sorting out to bring her closer.

Louise had volunteered at the reception. Jenny, the neighbour, was expecting her to, she could see. One look at Nigel would tell you that he never got his hands dirty. His hands were something she was shocked to recognise each time she saw him. They were still like a teenage boy's: bizarrely knuckleless and smooth. They made him look unprepared for life, despite his suit. Anyway, sorting out was a daughter's job.

'Oh, bless you,' Jenny had said, too relieved for even a token objection. 'Patrick's been saying just to put it all in bin bags, but really . . .'

There was everything to be done. At least the bed next door where her mother had died had been stripped, thankfully. It must have been Jenny, or the nurse. The bed in this room, the one Patrick slept in, needed changing. The pungent, old-man smell of the sheets permeated the room, although without, Louise was relieved to notice, anything urinal. It didn't help that there was something wrong with the radiator, which belted out unstoppable heat. The low-ceilinged bedroom was sweltering, even with the window sashes pushed as far up as they would go. Louise sweated as she worked; it was surprising how heavy clothes could be on their hangers. She was starving, but that was good. Work a bit off her. Burger and chips: the chewy fat of the burger and its salty blood mixing with the salty chips, sweet blob of ketchup. Maybe they could go to the pub for lunch. There was nothing in the house.

Louise hauled out a little run of formal clothes in yellowed dry-cleaning shrouds. Her mother must have stopped going to do's long ago—Louise knew Patrick had never been keen. Only once, after Mum had run off with Patrick (as Auntie B liked to call it, as though they were still running, cartoon-like), she had sent a photo of the two of them at some London party, a reception or ceremony, montaged with the famous. Patrick might have been getting an award, Louise couldn't remember. What she remembered was how glamorous the two of them had looked in the picture, Patrick and Mum, like old-fashioned film stars among the real film stars, both laughing. Patrick must have won something, or been expecting to, to be laughing for the cameras like that. Her mother had probably been wearing one of these dead dresses shoved beyond the coats. Louise remembered sparkles, flaring against the flash.

Hefting the heavy clothes on to the bed, she sneezed at the

resulting explosion of dust. Jenny's hints at the funeral about the state the house was in had been, like the woman herself, conservative. Other peoples' houses were always filthy—Louise was prepared for that—but as well as the enamel in the bathrooms (as yellowed and disastrous as Patrick's teeth), the ravaged paintwork (smeared with track lines of fingerprints, as if tracing the unsteady routes of a gigantic toddler), the dulled carpets (darker at the edges, where years of scamped hoovering had deposited tidal rings of dirt), there was the mess.

'Oh my days, Mum. It's like one of them programmes,' Holly had said when they arrived that morning.

With Patrick's study as the unseen epicentre, books, papers and bottles strewed the house like the aftermath of a disaster. It didn't look as though they'd thrown anything away in thirty years, not if you could read it. Next to the study, in the formal dining room, books and magazines were heaped so densely that they threatened the fragile-looking antique furniture with collapse. Moving out along the corridor, more printed matter was rammed horizontally into any space left in the packed bookshelves and bookcases, with more volumes stacked optimistically next to and in front of the housed editions, narrowing most thoroughfares to a precarious single file. Freestanding piles of books and papers teetered on stairs and landings, while others, typically near chairs in many rooms, had been adopted as permanent surfaces on which cairns of crumbed plates and unopened junk mail were balanced. Even the extra bedrooms, with the exception of the one where Louise's mother had died, were colonised by reams of hoarded print.

The bottles followed a more haphazard pattern, with the exception of the dark kitchen. Here, empties of varying sizes and colours had been serried in rows around the bin and along the wall as far as the dresser, in a display of historic consumption as formally impressive as an art installation or a tomb offering from an ancient civilisation. Only the bedroom came close to containing as many, although Louise had yet to see the study, Patrick's most private domain. He always kept the door closed.

So this was where Mum had lived, and how. Louise's memories of their childhood, pre-Patrick home were of irritably enforced cleanliness and order: knick-knacks that were purged of dust every few days, coasters that protected table surfaces, Mum advancing on rooms spraying Mr. Sheen ahead of her like tear gas at a riot. It seemed that much had changed. Of course Mum had been ill, as it turned out. For how long, though?

Turning to the mounded clothes on the bed, Louise could hear the sound of the TV from downstairs: Holly and Patrick were watching *Homes Under the Hammer* together. There was a tiny room off the corridor from the kitchen, like a nest, with a sagging sofa and tired cushions and years of scattered Sunday supplements, all arranged around a huge, spanking new flat-screen. It felt like the most inhabited room in the house, and was certainly the most inviting. There was a dust-dimmed gallery of framed photos on the shelves that surrounded the TV, mostly of Patrick or Patrick and Mum together, none of them recent. Helping Holly to find the remote, Louise had scanned the shelves and quickly killed the small hope of discovering any pictures of herself. In one, the oldest photo and the only one without Patrick, her mum was a young woman, holding Nigel as a blurred baby on her miniskirted knee, before Louise existed. It must have been the only photo she'd taken with her when she left.

It was getting to be late for lunch, and Louise needed a break. They also needed to decide what they were doing: she and Holly had brought their bags from the B and B so that they could get straight to the train, but if they went at three there would be stacks left undone. Louise really couldn't afford to stump up for another night away, and she wasn't entirely secure about the status of her return on the train. But supposing they stayed here in the house—could she really trust Jamie to get himself up in the morning? Not that it was the end of the world if he overslept; he was only doing work experience.

Patrick would never agree to it, probably.

'Where's Patrick?'

Down in the den, Holly was alone in front of the flat-screen, cradling her phone. She shrugged.

'How are you feeling, chick?'

She shrugged again. It wasn't like her not to be hungry. Ordinarily she'd be shouting the house down about needing her lunch by now. Poor little thing. She still looked pale.

Louise went to the study door and knocked. When there was no answer, she opened it to find Patrick at his desk, smoking, a whisky bottle to hand.

'Sorry to disturb you.'

No lights blinked in the housing of the ancient nicotine-beige computer that sat to his right. Its screen was equally lifeless. There was no other sign that he was writing, not so much as a piece of paper in front of him. Just the ashtray, the bottle and the glass.

'I don't want anything,' he said.

'Oh.' It hadn't occurred to her that he might want anything. She took up the cue. 'I could make you a coffee. Or I was wondering about going out to get a bit of lunch.'

He didn't respond to this.

'Patrick . . .'

His hair stuck up at the back, in need of a cut as well as a wash. There was still a lot of it. Louise remembered her mother pushing it back off his face, where it always fell. Adoring him.

'You don't look anything like her,' he said. 'You never have.'

'No.' Louise waited a second or two. 'I'm making headway, but there's quite a bit to do . . .'

'Burn the fucking lot, as far as I'm concerned. Put me on the pyre and have done.'

What was she supposed to say to that?

'Well. Even if it's the charity shop, they'll be grateful for it. It'll take me a little while yet, though.'

He drank. The whisky bottle was from Sainsbury's: 'Basics,' said the label.

'Would it be all right for Holly and me to stay the night? I could make up one of the beds—I mean, we'd share. That way everything would be sorted for you—I can talk to Jenny, is it, make sure . . . I mean, if you want someone to come in and . . . maybe just once a week, sort things out. Maybe you've got someone . . . I'll ask Jenny, shall I?'

'Nigel said he'd take care of the legal stuff.'

'I meant in the house.'

Patrick didn't move, except to take the glass a small distance from his lips.

'So we'll stay then, just for tonight. I'll bring something back for your lunch. You might fancy it later.'

The look Patrick wheeled to give her as she closed the door was violent and unfathomable. But it was as Louise remembered, from his visits to see her with Mum: the turning away, back to the glass and the bottle, did most of the damage.

She'd left her bag up in the bedroom. When Louise opened the door back into the unnatural heat, an impossible movement by the bed caught the edge of her eyeline, escaping with a weightless sigh. Even as she told herself not to be so stupid, her feet met an uncanny resistance. Starting back, she lost her balance.

Righting herself heavily against the side of the bed frame, Louise saw what it was that had moved against her; the draught from the opening door had agitated a wisp of dry-cleaning plastic that had come untethered from the neck of its hanger when she had heaped it with the others. It lay on the musty carpet, where it had drifted against her panicking feet. Stretching down, she squirmed to trap it, but it flounced limply away. She caught it on the second attempt. Her pulse returning to normal, Louise stood and hooked the plastic back over the hanger. *Stupid.*

It was as she shimmied the sheath down over the unprotected dress that she saw what the clothes had been trying to tell her all morning. Briskly, excited, she walked next door into the spare bedroom and opened the wardrobe there. Sure enough. A row of clothes, feminine, everyday, more recently worn than the spangled outfits abandoned in the room where Patrick slept. All the mess had stopped her thinking clearly; it would do the same to anyone. But the message was obvious, if you had eyes to see. Mum was telling her, loud and clear. Patrick said that they only knew about the cancer a week before she passed. Not enough time to get her and Nigel down to say goodbye. But Mum had been sleeping in the other room for months.

It was hard to be surprised he'd lie to them.

Cobham Gdns
April. 9? 10? '78
Sometime in the middle of the night

My darling—

I love you, I love you, I love you. You make me a better man than I ever thought possible, even the thought of you when I'm here in this desperate room marking desperate bloody essays about 'English countryside' for the Jap students. I can just about bear to work but it's impossible to read the newspapers without wanting to step in front of traffic. You're very sensible never to read them but then you seem wise about so many things. Beautiful and wise and irresistible. For all those reasons, your name can't be Sally.

Have your excuse ready for Wednesday. I've wangled the money for the ticket.

P xx

Two days after the funeral, Nigel was taken aback to ring Patrick and get Louise on the phone. At first he thought he'd dialled her number by mistake.

'We're back home tonight,' she told him. 'There's been that much to do.'

This was annoying, after all he'd been doing himself.

'You should have told me,' he said. 'I could have arranged to get someone in.'

'It's family,' she maintained. 'I've sorted a few things out you might like, or Sophie, you know, to have.'

Nigel couldn't imagine Sophie wanting anything from that grotto of a house. Unless—had there been jewellery? He remembered rings, catching light.

'How's Patrick?' he asked, more or less knowing the answer to that. He needed to speak to him, however fruitlessly. Assimilating the contents of the will, of which Nigel was co-executor along with Patrick's solicitor, it had become apparent that ownership of *Bloody Empire* had been transferred to their mother, for long-defunct tax reasons. Although clear provision had been made for the rights to the play to be transferred back to Patrick in the event of his wife's death, Nigel needed his consent. At the very least, it would make Patrick liable once again for any tax accruing. Then there was the matter of the house. That looked like it would be, as houses always were, rather more complicated.

Was *Bloody Empire* still put on anywhere? Nigel had been seventeen when he'd seen it, on the West End press night. He remembered best being allowed a gin and tonic in the bar at the interval. And the topless scene, naturally. He'd been permitted to come up from school specially, in the middle of the week in the middle of the term, and had greatly enjoyed the glamour on his return; underplaying it, but careful to mention the tits and exaggerating their, in truth, disappointing size and trajectory. They had been very political breasts, bracketed by underarm hair. That time was long gone, thank God. Nigel had been surprised to spot the actress in a *Poirot* a few years ago, much aged as a sadistic headmistress who became the murder victim, the breasts he had once ogled heavily covered in bloodstained tweed.

Patrick didn't come to the phone when Nigel rang. Louise said he was sleeping, in his study. (A study, now that was something to have.) They arranged for Nigel to ring back later in the day, before she and Holly left for their train. When Nigel called again, towards four, the phone rang on for so long he thought it was a lost cause. No answer machine kicked in, although he knew there was one because it had been the main conduit of communication between him and his mother when she was alive. Just as he was about to hang up, Louise answered, out of breath from the stairs. She then toiled to get Patrick.

'Do what you must,' was his response to Nigel's crisp summation of the rights situation. His voice sounded so thick with age and drink that Nigel faltered at the prospect of asking anything to do with the house. He wasn't even confident Patrick had understood what had just been so concisely put to him about his play.

'If you don't take measures to retrieve the rights,' he repeated, to be on the safe side, 'they'll pass to Louise and me.'

'She's still here,' said Patrick, distractedly. 'Turned the place out from top to bottom. I want her gone.'

'They're getting the train,' Nigel reassured him.

But after the conversation had finished, Louise rang him back on her mobile.

'I'm in the garden,' she told him. 'I don't want him to hear. Nidge, I don't think I should go.'

Nidge. It grabbed him. She didn't even know she was doing it.

Someone had turned up. A young woman. She claimed to be a

freelance journalist who had apparently some time ago arranged, via email, to interview Patrick. She seemed to be expecting to stay in the house, according to Louise.

'You know what journalists are like,' she said, groundlessly. As if she had ever had anything to do with journalists.

'Well, doesn't she know about Mum?' Nigel asked.

Apparently the girl hadn't, until she had arrived. And she had travelled down from Newcastle, or Sunderland, or possibly the Lake District—somewhere far north.

'What kind of freelance journalist?' he asked.

'I don't know. Or did she say she was studying journalism? Something like that. I couldn't really make it out, to be honest.'

This was impossible. Louise was hopeless on real-life details. That was the problem with never having to function in the real world, and God knows, Patrick was no better. But she had been right to warn him. Mum had always been the gatekeeper: now that responsibility had passed to him. The timing could have been better. Nigel had a big client presentation in the morning and the PowerPoint material wasn't yet finished for him to check over, while Sophie's annoyance over his absences from the house was cashing out in escalating acts of martyrdom he'd be stupid to ignore. That morning she'd even washed his gym kit for him and presented it to him at the door when he'd left at sparrow's fart: he knew the danger signs. She needed some attention. No wonder his IBS was playing up.

'Can you get her to ring me?'

Apparently the girl had wandered off, Louise didn't know where. She said she'd do her best. Nigel agreed that in that case it would be a good idea for Louise to stay if she could, until he could travel down after his presentation the next day. With Mum gone, who knew what some opportunist hack might be hoping to dig up? Patrick hadn't been newsworthy since 1982, but you never knew. A journalist could probably manipulate him into saying a story's worth of anything, if they were really that desperate for material. And at least being down there would allow him to have a proper conversation with Patrick about the future.

When Nigel got home that evening, Sophie had not only made coq au vin, but insisted the boys wait so that they could all eat it together. They were peevish and argumentative with hunger and tiredness. Nigel felt the same way, but he made a great effort to be charming and interested, and to praise the food, which he knew his digestion would suffer for later. As Sophie told an extended anecdote about her tribulations in returning some catalogue purchases, Nigel used the time to think through tomorrow and its compartments, starting with the presentation and moving on to whatever he would face in Cornwall. Perhaps it had worked out for the best that he'd be down there before Louise went for good: for all he knew, she might have stripped the house bare. Had there been rings? Sophie would remember. According to the will, he and Louise were to split everything evenly, but it would hardly be surprising if Louise took the opportunity to line her pockets while she could.

As he nodded at Sophie's detailed account of her interactions with various unhelpful courier agencies, Nigel checked this thought. Actually, it would be nothing short of astonishing to find Louise in breach of her stolid honesty: Nigel might have liked her so much more if she had ever in her life summoned enough gumption to steal, or even lie. Still, he'd confer with Sophie about the rings. As for the matter of Mum's title to the house, there was obviously no point in filling Louise in with the larger picture until it was entirely clear. Larger pictures overwhelmed her, they always had. She was vexed enough by a life lived in details.

'So they said of course we'll send a credit note and I said, you know what? You can send me a voucher for twenty-five per cent off and free delivery and maybe I won't post a moan on your website—course, I've already put it up.'

'Well done that woman.' Nigel patted Sophie's hand and accepted seconds on the coq au vin. Already, his guts were twisting.

The next day was predictably draining. On the train, Nigel made calls and formulated emails to compensate for his absence, both actual and prospective. Still, a refreshment-trolley cappuccino's length of staring out at the meaningless countryside was enough to drive him back to his laptop and its demands. Relaxation never helped; for one thing, it made him oversensitive to the alerts of his treacherous digestive system. The cappuccino had been a mistake, if you were to believe the nutritionist Sophie had arranged for him to see: no caffeine, no wheat, no dairy, no alcohol. Sod that. All the consultation had done was make him feel anxious about ignoring the prim, clear-skinned young woman's impossible advice, which probably made the symptoms worse. She had told Nigel the problem was that human evolution was much slower than the changes human beings had wrought on themselves with post-industrial nutrition.

Nigel didn't share his own theory: that his digestive system was the victim of a more personal failure to evolve. His belly had started to ache the moment he was removed from the carelessly processed diet of his childhood and forced to consume the grains and pulses and alien vegetables of his unusually progressive boarding school. By the time he had finished A-levels, the general middle-class diet had caught up with the headmaster's pioneering, yogurt-manufacturing wife and he was condemned to a lifetime of discomfort. Only in his student years had he found respite, confirming that existing on a diet of white-bread golden syrup sandwiches, Pot Noodles and bags of crisps eased the cramps and torrential shittings that otherwise tormented him. Sophie wasn't having it; she said it was all in his mind and forced him to eat courgettes as an example to the boys.

At the station Nigel took a cab, resenting the expense. When he arrived the house looked deserted, with no lights on, but it turned out that this was because everyone was in the kitchen at the back, eating. Everyone being Patrick, Louise, Holly (he had forgotten about her again) and the journalist, who introduced herself as Mia.

'Hi!' the girl exclaimed, as though welcoming him. As though his arrival had made her day. Having prepared to be defensive, Nigel was stirred to be winning. She was very attractive. She had glossy black hair and tight jeans and boots and looked a touch, a pleasing touch, oriental.

'I'm so sorry about your mother.'

Nigel made the noise and pulled the face suitable to acknowledging bereavement. He stopped Louise from fetching him a plate, explaining he'd had a sandwich on the train (actually, a palliative bag of salt and vinegar crisps). Patrick, whom he'd been expecting to look besieged, was convivial. Perhaps it was the right time of day, with the wine on the table. And the tight jeans.

'This charming young lady is here to pick what passes for my brains these days,' Patrick announced. As Louise rolled Nigel a look about this, she noticed Holly's plate, still full of glutinously overcooked pasta.

'Holly, you've got to eat something.'

'I told you—I'm not hungry. Can I get down now?'

She scarcely looked to be wasting away. Louise sighed and told her there were yogurts. The girl, ignoring this, got up without looking back and slouched out of the room, already texting. Her departure allowed Nigel to sit next to Mia.

'Yes,' said Nigel. 'Which paper are you from?'

Mia laughed. 'If only. I'm a student. I'm writing my thesis on—on Patrick.'

A little bow of the head to Patrick acknowledged the recent privilege of using his first name. Patrick dipped his head back, receiving the tribute. Nigel remembered that he could be charming.

'It's not an interview, then.'

Bloody Louise.

'I thought you said—' Louise objected.

'Well, it's a little bit two birds with one stone. Is that really awful? I was thinking—horse's mouth, for the thesis—sorry, that sounds terrible'—the girl flashed an even-toothed smile of contrition at Patrick—'but then maybe something for the student paper, if that's okay. I feel awful about the timing and everything.'

But not so awful that she hadn't got her feet under the table.

'Life of a sort goes on,' Patrick reassured her.

Nigel moved himself to be suspicious. 'Which university?' he asked.

'Newcastle.'

'You're doing a BA . . .'

'MA.'

'In—'

'Media and communications.'

Patrick snorted into his wine glass. This was all very awkward. Nigel thought the girl looked like she almost certainly was a student, although she seemed very groomed and self-confident. Young people were now though, weren't they? She could be any age from twenty to thirty. She could be a journalist, and lying through her teeth.

'I'm really so sorry about your mother; she was so nice to me when I emailed. I was really looking forward to meeting her. I should've double-checked or rung—it was just—I didn't think. Stupid of me.'

'It was all very sudden,' said Louise emphatically.

If only she hadn't come from so far away.

'Listen,' said Nigel, 'this isn't ideal, obviously. Why don't we reimburse you for your fare or petrol, or whatever, and you can arrange with Patrick to come down in a month or two?'

Patrick reared at this. 'Why the hell should she? The poor girl's here now.'

'Well—'

'Course, totally, I'm really sorry about all this—'

'It's not your fault, God—'

'Don't listen to this lot—'

'About inconveniencing you—'

'You aren't.' Patrick was definitive. 'I'm not inconvenienced. It's a delight to have you here. What did you arrange with Sara?'

Mia's eyes flicked around the three of them, assessing hierarchies.

'That I'd come and talk to you. She offered for me to stay . . . she said it wouldn't be a good idea to talk for more than a couple of hours at a time, because of your work. I mean, it started when I emailed—I just wanted to email you the questions, but she said you don't do email?'

'I prefer the old ways.'

'Yeah. So . . . it wouldn't be like, days.'

He could check the computer, thought Nigel. The emails would give him some sense of the girl's credibility, along with ringing the university. For now, he may as well keep Patrick sweet.

'Holly has to get back to school,' Louise said suddenly. No one could see the point of this. 'If you're wanting me.' No one wanted her. 'Maybe you should book yourself into the B and B up the road,' she said to Mia. 'I mean, tonight's okay, but after that. With the house. Patrick's not . . . there's no one to cook or anything.'

'Oh, I could do that,' said Mia. 'I love to cook. Don't get much chance at uni!'

She really was hot to trot, wasn't she?

Louise's face set. 'I suppose it wouldn't matter to keep Holly off until the end of the week. She's still a bit off-colour. Then I can see to you all.'

'You heard the girl,' said Patrick. 'She'll see to me.'

The innuendo eddied, unintended.

'I feel awful,' Mia repeated, her poise unassailed. 'Look, you're right, Mr Conway—'

'Nigel, please. It's not Conway, I'm his stepson—it's Dean, actually. But Nigel.'

'Oh God, sorry, duh, Mia. Listen, I'll go back in the morning, don't worry about the fare—'

'Stay!'

Patrick slammed the tabletop so hard that the plates jumped. They all stilled. Nigel felt he should be taking command of the situation, but he could never thump anything like that. In the ensuing silence, his stomach bubbled appeasingly. It was a small mercy, he realised, that his hay fever hadn't made a reappearance.

'We'll stay until Friday, then,' said Louise. 'It's not a problem.' She smiled, forcing her mouth. 'Does anyone fancy a yogurt?'

There were no takers.

May 19, 1978
Cobham Gdns

Dearest -

You're still on my lips, salt and sour and sweet all at once. I hope you missed your train and he knows what you've been doing and the whole world knows. I live for the taste of your cunt.

Leave him—and the children—and live with me. It's the only way, you know it is.

I love you.

P x

PS. If he tells you that, he's a liar.

THE VACUUM CLEANER was broken. With all Mum's clothes and bits sorted, Louise had decided to make a start on the house. It was nearly overwhelming, the amount there was to do if she was going to make a proper job of it. She assembled her materials: bucket, bleach, polish, dusters, rolls of paper towels. But the broken vacuum cleaner was a problem. There was no point discussing it with Patrick, or suggesting he fork out for a new one, although he'd have to eventually. She decided to call on the neighbour, Jenny, to see if she minded lending hers for the day. Holly could have done with the fresh air as well, but she refused to come with her. She still looked peaky, so maybe she was better off in the warm, thumbs busy on her phone.

'I'm just popping out.'

Patrick was in his study, answering Mia's questions. Louise had made them both a coffee. There should have been biscuits, but she had eaten them all herself watching TV the night before with Holly. By the look of her, Mia didn't go in much for biscuits. She even took the mug of coffee gingerly, as though its proffered handle was a mild, surprising insult she was graciously prepared to overlook.

'Honest toil,' said Patrick. Louise wasn't sure if this was getting at her or talking about him and the girl, who sat with her laptop angled on her crossed legs, tapping in notes. She closed the door on them, quickly.

It was a strange time, she thought, walking up the black unpavemented road to the other house. The countryside, that was strange in itself. Louise couldn't remember being in the country ever, really, apart from the odd school trip, although there was plenty of countryside around Leeds. Different from this: less something, or more something else—green? Up and down? There was the sea, as well, making it even stranger. She wondered if her mother, a Leeds girl all her life, had loved it. She must have, to have lived here nearly thirty years. Although she had loved Patrick enough to have been happy in a cardboard box. Those had been her exact words, Louise remembered that: her frozen to the stairs, her mum and dad rowing in the lounge, Dad shouting, 'Where are you going to live?' and Mum shouting back, 'What does it matter where we're living—I'd be happy in a cardboard box!' Luckily, it had never come to that.

The neighbour's house was chasteningly smart, with a gravelled drive and twin bay trees, pruned into lollipops, on either side of the matt, sage-painted front door. Jenny answered the bell, harried and pleasant and less forbidding than her paintwork.

'Oh, Sara's daughter—of course, come in!'

Sara. With the long 'a', like 'Baa, Baa, Black Sheep'. Louise never called Mum that, to herself. Sara was Patrick's invention; he had hated Sally and changed it. Since Louise had been here, she'd had to get used to attaching the other name to her mother, and to hearing herself say it, just to be understood. Auntie B had always stuck to calling Mum Sally, to make a point.

Louise, apologising for the intrusion, explained about the hoover. Jenny insisted she come in. Louise felt a right lump in that lovely house. Even by her standards, it was well looked after, and the furniture was gorgeous. Exactly the sort of thing she might have had herself if she'd been able to afford it, although she would have gone for a bit more colour than the chilly whites and beiges and greys that toned in so well with Jenny's thick ash hair and layered jumpers. Even the dog, an amiably overweight golden retriever, matched. Except for the house's size, it all couldn't have been more different from Patrick's and her mother's place.

'How is Patrick?'

Jenny led Louise into a pristine kitchen-diner with a granite-topped island in the middle. Radio 4 muttered to itself in the background.

'Not too bad. Well, taking it quite hard, really.'

Louise could hear her accent landing flatly on the granite in a way she never did at home. 'I'm not sure how he's going to manage, to be honest.'

Jenny sighed. 'No. It must be a worry.'

She wasn't going to join in, or help. Louise couldn't blame her.

'I thought I might—I don't think they had a cleaner—'

'No, I think there was a lady who retired—or maybe Patrick let her go.'

Jenny used the slender edge of her hip to nudge open a glossy white façade, revealing an immaculately ordered utility cupboard. 'I could pass on the number for ours—she's marvellous, but I don't know if she has a gap—she's rather in demand.'

She wheeled out the vacuum cleaner, which she insisted on emptying. Quickly establishing that it resembled nothing she'd ever pushed around a floor, Louise thanked the other woman for the trouble.

'I was very fond of your mum.' Jenny ran the tap to chase dust down the sink. 'I wish there had been more we could do.' The definitive sparseness of this statement clearly held so much more than its words that Louise immediately itched with questions. When? What was wrong? What were you hoping to do? Do you mean her being ill, or something with Patrick, before then? Why do you think the house was in that state? But it wasn't easy to talk to Jenny, through the barrier of cashmere and granite and Radio 4.

Carefully, the woman clicked shut the casing on the waste compartment. 'She told me all about you and your brother.'

Louise looked down to mask her welling eyes as Jenny tactfully concentrated on the vacuum cleaner.

'Let me give you a lift back. It's a heavy old beast.'

Throughout the short drive to the house, they both talked at slightly desperate length about the idiosyncrasies of the hoover. Louise promised to return it as soon as she'd finished, and when she'd turned off the car engine, Jenny asked her to read out the cleaner's number from her mobile, as she didn't have her reading glasses. Louise had to hold the mobile at arm's length to see the digits while Jenny wrote them down for her. She probably needed glasses herself: another thing that needed sorting.

'She did—' Jenny hesitated. 'I do think your mother would have wanted to speak to you, if things had been different. She got worse so quickly . . .'

'You didn't know, then?' Louise asked. 'That she was ill?'

'No,' said Jenny. 'I don't think anyone did, did they?'

Louise wished she could confide in her about her suspicions regarding Patrick and the separate bedrooms, but she was dumb with everything else she wanted to ask Jenny, who had known Mum so much better than her. She declined her offer of help to wrestle the hoover out of the back seat. Blurting a final thank you, she carried the contraption inside. She was desperate for a cup of tea and something to eat. But as soon as she got in, she could hear shouting—Patrick and Holly, coming from the upstairs landing. The girl, Mia, stood at the foot of the stairs; retreating or advancing, it was impossible to tell. She smiled at Louise, absolving herself, as Louise rushed up to see what was going on. Holly's appeal to her was immediate.

'I didn't do nothing!'

'Get out!'

Patrick was purple, beside himself. Louise stepped in before he could hit Holly, although for all his rages she'd never seen him do violence.

'He chucked the radio—he's broke it! I didn't do nothing, promise, Mum!'

Through the open door of the bathroom, Louise saw Patrick's elderly radio on the floor, its roar of untuned static adding to the chaos. The approach of her body as she went to retrieve it provoked a flare of deafening interference. She twisted the dial, greasy with antique filth, until it clicked off.

'You're mental, you!'

'Holly, that's enough.' Quickly, Louise moved back on to the landing. 'What's been going on?'

Holly had been running a bath, and, as she explained, since she couldn't listen to music on her phone in case it dropped in, had decided to use the radio instead. Patrick had apparently gone berserk at the noise. He'd said that it was impossible to work with that deafening crap playing at top volume, he couldn't hear himself think in his own house, he'd had enough of both of them, they should fuck off and leave him alone and he wanted no more to do with them. And more along those lines, as Holly sobbed.

'Patrick, she didn't think. She's not fourteen till next month.'

'I can see that thinking doesn't come easily—'

'Holly, apologise to Patrick.'

'I didn't do nothing!'

'Say you're sorry.'

'What for?'

'Holly.'

Mia spoke from the stairs. Her low voice was hypnotically calm.

'Patrick—sorry—I think we were ready to take a break anyway, weren't we? Sorry. Can I make everyone some lunch?'

At Mia's suggestion, Patrick meekly agreed to a lie-down until the food was ready. As the rest of them went downstairs, Mia apologised to Louise with insincere diplomacy: it was probably all her fault, Patrick was probably tired out from all the morning's talking. Louise started to make tuna sandwiches, insisting that Mia sit down when she started faffing round her, offering to help. Holly was back on her phone, texting, probably to tell her friends about Patrick's meltdown.

'It's such a lovely house,' said Mia. Like everything she said, it sounded as though she was repeating something she had been asked to learn. Or it might just have been good manners. Through the recent filter of Jenny's tactful good taste, Louise felt an ancient embarrassment in her association with the house, its rundown state and the abnormalities of its household.

'It needs looking after.'

'Oh, I don't know. It's sort of exactly like you imagine a writer's house to be, all nooks and crannies and books and stuff . . . atmosphere.'

'Rank,' Holly remarked, bent over her phone.

Mia accepted her plate with the sandwich on with the same air of faint, gracious surprise with which she'd taken her coffee. She offered to go and fetch Patrick, but Louise told her to leave him; he could have his sandwich whenever he was ready and he might well be asleep now. She wondered if he'd finished the bottle she'd found in his room when she was clearing it. 'Basics' again.

'Hasn't he been sleeping at night?' asked Mia, all synthetic concern. Louise told her that she had no idea. The three of them ate on. Mia, Louise noticed, left her crusts.

'I couldn't turn it off,' said Holly, finally finishing with her phone and assuming the conversation was where her attention had last left it. She was talking about the radio. 'I turned the knob thing when he started going into one and it wouldn't turn off.'

'Maybe you'd got the volume by mistake,' said Louise. 'They're funny, those old radios.'

'It's right spooky,' Holly insisted. 'You can feel it upstairs, near where me grandma died. It's freaking me out.'

Mia tucked her hair behind her ears, two sleek commas. 'The radio must be like broken or something?'

Louise recognised the set of Holly's face. Mia had no idea how stubborn she could be. 'It's not, I told you. It's weird. Summat's going on up there.'

Mia smiled. 'You must know there's no such thing as ghosts.'

Holly gazed back. 'Course there is. Everyone knows there is. It's like proved by scientists?'

Mia stood, gathering the plates and tipping her crusts into the bin.

'Haven't you seen *Most Haunted*?'

Mia said she hadn't. Holly sighed at Louise.

That night, from the way Holly cuddled up to her in the spongy bed they'd been forced to share, Louise could tell she was still fretting about the business with the radio.

'You know, your grandma . . . If someone passes, that's natural—in an old house like this lots of people must have died, if you think about it.'

'Oh, Jesus!'

The mattress lurched as Holly hitched back closer to her. Louise kissed the back of her neck, where the hair had slid away on to the pillow. It smelled of her, the same smell she'd had as a baby.

'Two more nights, that's all.'

Holly squirmed free. They settled, their breathing countered in a sequence that evaded rhythm, their pulses their own. It had been years since they'd shared a bed, except for the odd bad dream, and even those had stopped some time ago.

'Why didn't you ever see Grandma?'

Louise shifted, the disparity in their weights making Holly collapse against her in the lee of her body.

'I don't know, really. It was difficult living so far away.'

'We could have come for holidays,' Holly offered, after a pause to think about this.

'We hadn't fallen out. It was just . . . I suppose I had my life and she had her life, you know.'

'Are you sad she died?'

At this, Louise heaved around to face Holly with such force that Holly had to put out her arm to stop herself rolling on to the floor.

'What a stupid bloody question, of course I'm sad. She was my mother!'

She could see the frightened glitter of Holly's eyes in the dark. It wasn't her fault.

'When you're older, you might understand. Us not seeing each other . . . it was just one of those things. She loved Patrick very much. It was a—big love story.'

A few breaths, in in, out out, in out. 'But what about your dad?'

Frozen on the stairs, the awful sound of Dad crying in the lounge.

'What about him?'

'They were married, her and your dad.'

'These things happen, don't they?'

They turned away from each other to sleep, but it was Holly whose breathing stretched out first. Soon, she was so deeply asleep that even the buzz of an incoming text from beneath her pillow didn't wake her. What was she like? They never stopped. The noise, so close to her own ear, had nearly given Louise a heart attack. After that she stayed awake for what felt like hours, with the phone giving the occasional rasp, like a wasp dying on a windowpane. She was tempted to text Scarlett back and put the fear of God into her, but she wasn't confident of her way around Holly's phone and she'd never hear the end of it if she deleted something by mistake. Instead, Louise listened to the cracks and settlings of the house around her. You never knew. Concentration had never been her strong point, but she needed to start paying proper heed. Only two more days left. Maybe there was another message, somewhere, if she knew how to look. Hadn't Jenny said Mum would have wanted to speak to her?

Cobham Gardens
August 3rd, 1978

Dearest, Dearingest –

I bloody hate it. Please believe me when I say the last thing I want is another day like that, utter misery all round. I don't mean to hector—it's just knowing, as I said, how happy we could be, how happy you could make me, and seeing it squandered—your loveliness and lightness squandered. If not to me—and I believe you when you tell me you love me, ~~remembering your delicious shyness breaks—~~you surely owe it to yourself to make an attempt at happiness, instead of settling for chicken in a bloody basket. Oh, and the promise of a 'fitted kitchen'!!

You say I don't understand about the children but I do. It's not as though they're babies. ~~If you love me~~ Love demands sacrifice: it's as old as Abraham and Isaac. I'm not asking you to cut their throats. And I could afford to send your boy to school, think of that.

If I am to say anything to the world I need you with me to help me say it.

My Sara. My only Sara. Only my Sara. How I hate this stinking country. Tell me that's all you want, truly, and I'll leave you alone. Miserable. <u>Miserable</u>.

P xx

NOT LONG AFTER he'd turned out his reading light, Sophie's backside brushed luxuriantly against Nigel's leg. The deliberation of the contact stirred him from sleep's early drift. Now he was alert. Her buttocks made another pass, unmistakably. He put a hand on her hip and slithered her nightdress up to reach skin. Ten minutes before, she had given him a tongueless, terminating kiss goodnight and rolled gratefully into her pillow. Sleep was all she wanted. Something, he had no idea what, had happened to change this. Blindly reaching for his wife's breasts, Nigel pressed his thickened cock into the small of her back. He wondered if he could reach to switch the lamp on. Better not. She was more enthusiastic in the dark.

They moved in escalating, familiar ways, made stranger by the lack of light. Skin; hair; smells, natural and synthetic, some unique to Sophie, some shared between them. After their twelve years together, sex was like a flow chart with limited possible outcomes. If yes, then proceed to step four, if no, continue with step three . . .

'Condoms?'

'Drawer.'

As Sophie reached out to the bedside table, Nigel struggled to remove his pyjama top. Maybe she'd put the lamp on now? But no, she preferred to scrabble around in the dark. As maintenance foreplay, he kissed his way down the back of her neck while she ripped open the foil sachet. Suddenly, a brutal arc of light sliced them across. Oliver's small silhouette stood at the open door. He sobbed, gathering momentum, as Nigel and Sophie froze in position like escaping PoWs in a war film.

'Sweetheart—'

Sophie hurried out of bed, her nightdress belling back down to unflattering mid-calf, and scooped him up.

'Was it a bad dream?'

The little boy clamped her gratefully, shins and ankles dangling from his outgrown pyjamas as she staggered him back across the hall to his bedroom. Nigel subsided. Ah, well. He moved back into his warmer patch of mattress, away from the hall light. Hopefully Sophie would turn it off when she was done with Olly. Both boys had nightlights, shaped like benign cartoon ghosts.

Ghosts. Nigel thought of his mother, dying in that dusty house. Her last nights. Had there been a light on for her? Had she been frightened? She had known, after all, that there was nothing to be done: it was Patrick the truth had been kept from in that last week. Nigel had had a phone conversation with the GP, following the results of the post-mortem necessary after any death at home. The doctor had reassured him that Sara had been medicated beyond any sort of pain. Easy enough for him to say that: who now could tell any differently? Apparently Mum had been 'most insistent' that Patrick not be told how ill she was. It was hard to say if this had been a kindness, in the end. Perhaps she had just wanted to be left in peace, without his imminent bereavement hijacking the arduous days of her dying.

Roaming around the house, and Patrick, and his mother, Nigel arrived at the thought of the student, Mia. He hadn't had time to check out her credentials; he must put that on his list for the following day. His dying hard-on quickened. There was something about her. So glossy. So young.

The hall light was still on. It was impossible to tell how long was Sophie going to be, comforting Olly back to sleep. Discreetly, Nigel began to bring himself off. Sometimes she got into bed with the boys until they were safely asleep, and fell asleep herself. But no, just as he was moving more urgently against his hand, Mia bent over the old table in the Cornwall kitchen, the hall light went out and Sophie scuttled back to their bed. Nigel rearranged himself as she put her newly freezing feet his way.

'Thought we were out of the woods with him waking up,' she said. 'I hope he's not starting again.'

Nigel moved Sophie's icy hand downwards, just to let her know. It stayed for a second, gave his crotch a neutering pat and returned to the heat of his chest. All she wanted from him now was warmth. She wriggled against him.

'Maybe it's all, you know, with your mum.'

'It can't mean much to him.'

They had taken Oliver down to see Nigel's mother when he was a baby: this had been, come to think of it, their last face-to-face meeting with her. There had been similar plans to take Albie for a viewing when he was born, but the visit had been postponed for some reason to do with either Sophie or Mum, he couldn't remember which, and hadn't, finally, happened. His mother had never travelled to Surrey to see them. This was just understood. Sophie kept a sparse gallery of the cards Mum sent up on the fridge as a meagre corrective to those from her own mother, Ganny T, the overlaid strata of which regularly defeated the tenacity of the fridge magnets, but surely the boys were too small to take in, at any level, their other distant grandmother's death? It wasn't as though they'd seen Nigel emoting about it all over the place, because he hadn't been. He felt fine. He felt so fine he felt slightly irritable at the thought that it might not be normal to be so unaffected by the death of your mother. Or maybe the irritation was because he was horny. He really was. Although he also desperately needed to pee, which was confusing matters. Surely he was too young to be starting with prostate problems?

When he tried again with Sophie's hand, she pulled it away

and turned firmly on to her side. This decided him. He swung out of bed.

'I'll need to go down there again, I'm afraid,' Nigel said, heading for the en suite. 'Lay the will out for Patrick. Maybe you can come with the boys.'

Sophie moaned, already on her way to sleep. He knew this would be an unadopted suggestion. But at least he'd got it in there, as he'd remind her tomorrow when he firmed up her refusal. It suited everyone for him to go to Cornwall alone. Nigel wondered if Mia would be gone by the weekend. Probably.

When he'd finished in the bathroom (everything seemed normal, but maybe he'd book in for a prostate check), he made his way downstairs to the computer. There were things to do, as always. He had been deliberating about whether to let his father know about Mum. Well, Dawn, his second wife. Dad had been holed up in a home in Stockport for nearly ten years, deterioratingly vacant with Alzheimer's. Digging out Dawn's address—she had no email—Nigel recognised the self-serving tidiness of the gesture. If his father had been alert to the world, he wouldn't have welcomed news about Mum. He'd tried hard to keep her, but once she'd gone, he never mentioned her again. And he had passed the two of them, his first children (there were two more sons, with Dawn), on like parcels. Louise to Auntie B, Nigel to the school Patrick had paid for. They were no more orphans now than they'd been thirty years ago, and nothing would change when Dad's body died as well as the rest of him.

Still, it would be better all round to let Dawn know. One of the duties and advantages Nigel had derived from being sent to public school was the civilising art of correspondence. Thank-you letters, notes of introduction, job applications, and now this. By the time the boys were grown up, making marks on paper would be an obsolete skill, along with whistling. But for now, it was poignantly appropriate, all the more so for calling on a formalising decency he was seldom asked to exercise. With a thought for his mother, who had made all this possible, Nigel opened the drawer that contained writing paper, took out the heavy sheets, and found his pen. She, of course, never wrote.

Headland Heights Hotel
Newquay
Cornwall
November 2nd 1978

Darling girl –

Forgive scrawl, wine at dinner trying to make grim surroundings less grim. The only other guests are businessmen in suits, here for some kind of conference. As house rules demand dressing for dinner (piss elegance), they assume I'm one of them. Some of the b'men dine with their 'secretaries', all of whom wear flimsy tops with no bra. Effect in freezing dining room like sitting among a convention of peanut smugglers. One though, scandalously, has brought his wife! (Nipples firmly covered, thank God.)

Pounding seas. Very cold here, and empty, and beautiful. I am cold and empty, but as you know, only beautiful in your eyes. Although there is a little chambermaid with big brown eyes and bigger tits who seems to have taken a fancy to me . . . her hospital corners when she makes my bed speak volumes. I might take a crack at her, since you're no longer interested.

I hope you don't mind me writing. ~~Hope the kitchen is all~~ Writing proper is torture, but am grinding out a scene or two on a good day (not every day is). The main character is a man possessed by a daemon—good or bad, I haven't decided, but she's certainly you. She's also Albion, the spirit of old England—you wouldn't believe some of the things that have come out of your mouth . . .

I do understand the phone is impossible, but if you cared to drop me a line, ~~it~~ I would be very grateful.

I'm the loneliest man in the world.

P xx

THE GARDEN HAD probably been lovely once. Louise thought she might remember it from a photo Mum had sent when she and Patrick first moved in: the two of them shaded under a patio umbrella, toasting their good fortune with a gaudy array of bedding plants saturating the background. Even now, with the grass patchy and high and the beds barely woken into spring, you could see how nice it would be with a bit of work, stretching out towards the sea. Talking to Jamie on her mobile, Louise used her free hand to pluck at the weeds clogging a row of paving stones. The stones wound down to a birdbath, its contours blurred with moss.

'Have you done any washing?' she asked him. He told her he didn't need any.

'What about pants? And socks and that?'

He didn't need any. Stooped over the path, Louise had a good view of the back of the house. The windows were in a shocking state. She could ask Jenny about a window cleaner.

'I hope you've been getting up.'

'Course I've been getting up.'

The school would let her know, if they could be bothered. Jamie was so close to leaving they'd more or less washed their hands of him, even with GCSEs still to come. No one was expecting him to cover himself with glory there.

'What's the place like?' she attempted. 'Work experience?'

Jamie had actually shown a bit of enthusiasm for that, the prospect of going into a joiner's and carpenter's for a week. He was good with his hands.

'Dunno. All right. Bit crap.'

He managed to communicate that the place at the joiner's had fallen through—he had no idea why—and in its place, the school had been sending him to an industrial dairy for the week.

'Oh well,' Louise said, unable to contribute any more on that subject. 'Only another couple of days, eh?'

At the end of the house, shadows behind the long window arch lurched, bouncing light from the glass. It was Patrick's study. He was in there having his last morning with Mia. She'd already booked the taxi to take her to the station, around five.

Louise couldn't manufacture any more questions once Jamie confirmed that he had enough money, and enough food in the house. She really wasn't needed. She promised to ring him at the same time tomorrow. He hung up first. Louise felt the lack of him, but then she felt that even when they were in the house together: his gangling remoteness, his silence that she wanted to break into in case it contained sadness. When he'd been a baby she used to kiss him and kiss him, all over, until he bubbled over with laughter. She loved to see him laugh now, cracking up at something stupid on the computer or on TV. It was never her who made him laugh any more, not on purpose, but maybe that was normal.

Louise got going on the path. She always liked to finish a job, and it was satisfying seeing the margins of the rounded stones appear from beneath the weeds. Patrick had made it clear that he didn't want her to do any more around the house. Which reminded her; she must return the hoover to Jenny.

'Mmmmmn . . .'

Mia stood on the back steps, taking in the air and stretching as though she wanted to be watched. Louise thought it might be yoga. On the upswing the stretches pulled the girl's top from her jeans, revealing her concave stomach and the top of her hip bones.

'Would you like a coffee?' Mia asked. When she returned to standing, her hair fell back perfectly, as though freshly brushed.

'Sorry—'

Louise, still holding her most recent handful of weeds, headed for the patio. It had become a routine over the last couple of days, her bringing in the coffee for Mia and Patrick. Talking to Jamie, she'd forgotten.

'No, I can make it,' Mia objected. 'Just wondered if you wanted one.'

'I'll do it. You're busy.'

'To be honest, I could do with a break.'

Even as she said this, Mia sat on the top step, levering down from the hip without moving her planted feet. That looked like yoga as well, or the result of it. Louise chucked the weeds into a waste patch vivid with grape hyacinths and continued past her towards the kitchen. When she brought back the tray a few minutes later, the girl took the mug in that way of hers, as though it was unexpected.

'Thanks so much!'

Since Mia made no move to go back to Patrick, Louise took his coffee in for him. In the moment before she knocked on the open door, Louise felt sorry for the hopeless drop of Patrick's shaggy head as it bent mechanically to the cigarette. (Mia had probably gone outside to escape the smoke.) As soon as she'd knocked, though, all her teenage nervousness returned. He barely looked round as she placed the mug at his elbow, and he didn't speak.

Turning away, Louise saw that a photo that sat on the desk, to the right of the kippered computer, was of her mother. The camera had come in close on her wearing a sort of crown of flowers and smiling with her eyes downcast. She didn't look like herself. It was only the goofy vampire points of her incisors that identified the smile as hers.

'It's Mum.'

Patrick turned, irritated by her exclamation. She wondered if he would allow her to take the picture so that she could look at it properly, but seeing him close his eyes against her, she decided not to ask. She could always come in when the room was empty. 'I've never seen that one before.'

Patrick lifted the frame from the desk, leaving the outlines of its lower edges stencilled in the surrounding dust. How many years since anyone had moved it? Bringing the photo briefly into range of his proper vision, he grunted, then cast it down, the sight unbearable to him. Unsupported by its angled brace, the picture lay prone on the desk's worn leather. Louise knew better than to rescue it.

Was it a wedding photo? That would explain the crown of flowers. It had only been Mum and Patrick at the wedding, as far as she knew. Dad had made the announcement, visiting her at Auntie B's. It must have been a good year after he'd decided he couldn't cope with her and Nigel, and Auntie B had stepped into the breach. Nigel had already been away at school for ages, so she had no one to share the news with. Not that Dad had produced it as news. Telling her that Mum was married was a weapon, designed to sever something. He had never mentioned her after that. Come to think of it, it must have been around then that he met Dawn and his visits began to peter out.

In the kitchen, Mia loitered with her empty mug. 'Thanks, Louise.' The girl made a point of rinsing the mug at the sink and putting it on the draining board, while humming unconvincing appreciation at the green light that shone in through the window from outside. She seemed to be wanting a conversation.

'Your mother must have loved the garden.'

Anyone with eyes to see could tell no one had loved that garden for a very long time. But had Mum taken care of it, at the beginning? The back garden in their Leeds terrace had been a tiny concreted square, fissured by weeds and mainly occupied by Dad's motorbike. Louise remembered now that Mum's excited litany when she and Patrick bought the house had included quite a bit about the garden's beauty and size. 'Is that what Patrick said?' she asked Mia.

Mia looked around for a tea towel and started to dry her mug. 'We've just been talking about his work, really. I imagine though, before she got ill . . .'

'She wasn't ill for very long. As far as any of us know.' Louise couldn't resist that bit. 'That's why it all came as a bit of a shock.'

'Oh. I'm sorry, I didn't . . .'

Louise saw that the girl was embarrassed. Maybe this was all she was, landing in the middle of them like this, and her way of talking was just her attempt to conceal it. She made an effort to match Mia's tone.

'You're right, though, she must have needed something to do while Patrick was in there writing all day!'

They smiled at each other. What *had* Mum done with all those empty hours? Certainly not housework.

'I don't have much idea what Patrick's been working on,' said Mia, 'do you? He hasn't had anything produced in years, has he? I mean, you know, theatre stuff.'

Louise didn't know. The girl looked uncomfortable, but impelled to speak. 'To be honest, I don't think he's actually written anything for ages.'

'Oh well,' said Louise. It wasn't for her to say.

During their conversation Holly had dawdled in. She was definitely well enough now to be back at school, although she was still going about with a face like a smacked arse. No doubt about it, Louise was looking forward to being back at home, whatever state they found it in.

'How many books has he written then?' Holly asked Mia. Mia looked surprised. Louise was surprised herself.

'Well, you know, they're plays.'

Holly looked indifferent. Anything written was a book to her. Mia smiled, a new expression, which made her much younger.

'To be honest, I'm not sure myself: I'll have to google it. I only really know the kind of famous one? The successful one, whatever. Not that many. Four? I think he wrote a few before.'

Holly had already lost interest.

'Amazing,' said Mia, trailing into silence.

Louise had tried to read *Bloody Empire* once, when the main library first got a copy. She had just left school, and was signing on. The fuss in the press was still quite recent. There was something magical about seeing Patrick's book installed on a shelf in municipal respectability—proof of her own connection to a much larger world. Louise remembered exactly the unthumbed thickness of the individual pages, the assertive black text, the shiny blue of the cover and its urgent black-and-white photo of some crouched, howling figure. She also remembered how impossible it had been to understand, despite how very much she'd wanted to, the collection of oddly named people talking. She'd never read a play, before or since. It had endorsed all her awe of Patrick's alien brilliance, the impossible air her mother breathed. Just for that time, there in the library, before she was defeated in her struggle to make sense of those baffling speeches and actions, Louise had felt that her life was going to be quite different.

'It's weird your mum not being an actress,' said Mia. Louise must have shown her surprise. 'Sorry, I don't know if it's horrible talking about her, or upsetting for you, I—'

'I don't mind,' said Louise. Who else was left to talk about her?

'I mean, she was very beautiful, from the pictures.'

Well, Mum had been very beautiful. Louise didn't even take after her dad, who hadn't been bad-looking himself—in his twenties, anyway.

'So I suppose I just thought that's how she and Patrick must have met, through her being in something of his . . .'

'No, nothing like that. I don't think she'd have been able to act her way out of a paper bag. She worked in a chemist after she got married. To my dad, I mean.'

'How did she and Patrick meet?'

'You'll have to ask Patrick,' Louise told her. 'I don't really know.'

Saying this, Louise's ignorance peeled away so that she could see it, spread out for her like one of those old maps that stopped where they thought you dropped off the edge of the world. She'd never really wondered, let alone asked. It was what came after that that had meant so much. Patrick and Mum had met. That was the beginning, and everything else had followed. It was an old story, and now only Patrick was left to tell it. Head over heels. That was all she knew, from Auntie B. They'd fallen head over heels. Like Jack and Jill. Except Jack and Jill had been brother and sister.

'It's probably a good story!' she said.

Mia, as usual, was looking at Louise as though she spoke in another language, one she was determined, without aptitude, to learn.

'I bet it's amazing,' she agreed.

Cobham Gardens
Tuesday night. December. (14??)

Oh God,

You're right, there's no point tormenting ourselves. Although torment with you is preferable to ordinary ecstasy with any of the others. Yes others, my love. A full and frank declaration, since you insist:

The chambermaid, as you know. No more to say.

A girl who works in my agent's office. Blackheads on her breasts and an appalling laugh. I was pissed. For her sake, I hope she was too.

Not quite Mrs Langley's Swiss or possibly Austrian au pair. Long pre-Raphaelite (look it up) hair, and legs all the way up. Interrupted only by her fear of discovery. We were in the Langleys' bathroom (a party), there isn't a proper lock.

But I only think of you. You you you. I went to another literary shitterary party last night and was preyed upon by a 40-year-old lady writer you won't have heard of who beds tyros like me as trophies. Not my type at all, although a celebrated beeyootay, so don't worry. I don't fancy her any more than I fancy ending up in her memoirs.

You will be the sole subject of mine, with or without you. No cheap cracks about the kitchen, please note.

Patrick x

The doctor says the reason I can't shift the cough is smoking, so trying to cut down. Hell.

Nigel hadn't intended to arrive unannounced on Saturday afternoon, but no one picked up the landline despite three attempts, and although he left a message on Louise's mobile, she didn't get back to him. The house was shut-off and dim as he paid the cab, its pall of unwelcome enhanced by the mizzle that filled the air like a teenage mood. If they were going to put the place on the market, and that 'if' was highly moot, and a very compelling reason to talk to Patrick, the whole lot would need much more than a lick of paint.

By now, he knew better than to present himself at the front. He went round to the kitchen, knocked for form's sake, and let himself in through the door that skewed down from its frame at the top.

The kitchen looked better for Louise's efforts, no doubt about it. With the bottle installation removed and surfaces scoured, you could appreciate the depth of the window frames and the solidity of the walls. For the first time, Nigel's imagination reached beyond estate agent's details to him and Sophie and the boys settled here, under mellow beams. A second home, why not? Plenty of the partners had them. For Sophie it would be a whole invigorating project—she loved that sort of thing. She'd never been happier than when tearing out the perfectly good bathroom in the house they'd bought when she was pregnant with Olly, replacing it to specifications uncompromised even by having to relieve her increasingly strained bladder in a bucket. It would be interesting to see what Patrick might say.

'Hello?' he tried. The house was silent. Nigel walked up the dark corridor that led from the kitchen, glancing into each low, cold room that led off it. The smell in the dining room declared a damp problem that got worse in the library, absorbed, no doubt, into the pages of all those books, which remained. The vast TV was dark in the den. No one ever went into what he supposed was called the drawing room, with its handsome chimney breast and rigidly opposed sofas. At the end of the corridor was Patrick's study. Approaching it, Nigel couldn't deny a tickle of fear. The uneven flags had resounded against his shoes with each step; if Patrick was in there, surely he must have heard him by now? His feet landed softly outside the shut door, where a cheap, newish rug marked the threshold. Nigel knocked, just in case.

The chair was pushed snugly into the desk, the computer off. The ashtray was empty. It was all a bit *Marie Celeste*. Nigel took out his phone and called Louise again. This time she answered, patchily.

'We're on the train!'

They'd left that morning, heading back to Leeds. Mia had gone the night before, disappointingly. But Louise was worried to hear that Patrick wasn't around: had Nigel checked upstairs? He couldn't have had a fall, could he? Maybe Nigel should—The line died. Nigel went upstairs, without ringing her back.

Nigel was relieved to find the bathroom clear of Patrick, as well as the bedroom. He briskly glanced into the other rooms, the one where his mother had died included, although he left it to last, and was perfunctory. Empty. There was no one in the house except him.

He rang Louise back.

'He isn't here. The back door was open.'

They wondered together what to do, although Nigel immediately regretted the collaboration. His sister told him to check the garden, as though he wouldn't have thought of it. After he had promised to do this, and to call her if Patrick turned up, she interrupted his sign-off to ask, 'Have you seen the curtains?'

'What curtains?'

'The ones in the room, you know, where Mum . . . not their bedroom, the other one.'

Since Nigel was standing just outside, he once again opened the door to the room where their mother had died. The curtains, drawn shut, were fudgy beige and unexceptional. Curtains were the kind of thing Sophie could spend hours on. From her beleaguered anecdotes, Nigel had picked up that they tended to be both problematic and expensive. It remained hard to see why.

'Yeah. What's the thing with the curtains?'

'They're new.'

Louise cut out again, but keenly rang him back to explain. If their mother had only become ill in the week or so before her death, as Patrick claimed, why had she been sleeping in the spare room long enough to warrant and allow the ordering of a new set of curtains? Nigel was baffled. He suggested, simply, that the curtains had been worn out and she had at some point replaced them. No mystery there.

'In that house?' said Louise. Nigel took the point. Their mother's deficiencies as a housekeeper apart, when did they ever have guests to warrant such an uncharacteristic effort?

'Anyway, her clothes. All her everyday clothes were in that room, Nidge. I realised when I was doing the sort-out. It was only the ones she didn't wear any more she kept in their ward—'

This time Louise seemed to have gone for good. Oh, she was an annoying cow. He had heard the excitement in her voice. Always latching on to something, milking it for emotion. If you could be passive aggressive, maybe it was possible to be a passive drama queen. What was it she was cranking up here? That Mum had been sleeping in the spare room for months because she was ill and Patrick had kept it from them? Even if he had, so what? It wasn't like he'd held a pillow over her face. And why had Louise chosen to delay sharing this speculation until she was well away from any possibility of confronting Patrick about it? If she felt so thwarted from a late-stage Florence Nightingale bid to care for Mum, she could take him on herself. Nigel certainly wasn't going to say anything.

A sound intruded: the tidal crunchings of a car labouring cautiously into the pocked drive. From the landing window, Nigel saw the livery of the local taxi firm. Patrick got out, fishing in his raincoat pocket for cash. He looked different. Smarter somehow, despite the raincoat. The cab drove off. Nigel headed downstairs.

'What are you doing here?'

Patrick's tone was amiable, despite his surprise. Nigel saw that he'd had a haircut. The flop of his forelock as he tossed the house keys into a dish on the hall table was newly boyish.

'I tried to ring.'

'They've all gone, thank Christ.' Patrick's ears, revealed by the trim, were enormous. Once Nigel had noticed this, it was difficult not to stare. Surely they hadn't always been that large? 'I suppose it's me you want?'

Nigel said that it was. Which was true, given everything there was to dot and cross. Certainly better to do it without the irritant of Louise, and perhaps even lacking the stimulant of Mia. He pointed out to Patrick that he'd left the back door unlocked.

'Nothing worth stealing,' he shrugged, leading the way in to the kitchen. He'd brought a pasty in from town, which he ate messily straight from the paper bag, while Nigel made them both an instant coffee and ferreted out a hardened stripe of cheese left in the anachronistically tiny fridge. *No caffeine, no dairy.* He completed the diabolical trinity with the heel of supermarket white sliced Louise had abandoned in the bread bin, making himself a sandwich.

'Do you think you'll stay here, Patrick?'

In the moment of delay before he answered, Nigel feared an outburst, but Patrick's shrug was amiable. A trip to the pub had possibly followed the barber's.

'I don't see why not. Managed here long enough.'

'Yes, but. It'll be different, won't it, without Mum, I mean?'

Patrick snorted, spraying crumbs. They both ate on. Now was the time to mention the house, the ownership of the house. Finishing his last mouthful, Patrick crumpled the empty paper bag and said, 'A pair of brown eyes.'

Nigel made a vague noise of agreement at this unprovoked reminiscence. Patrick hooked a finger in a back molar to retrieve a piece of gristle, which he wiped on the balled-up paper bag.

'Stupendous knockers.'

Nigel couldn't really continue the agreement. You couldn't think of your own mother's breasts as knockers. Had they, in any case, been all that stupendous? She had been rather a slight woman.

'Your mother was jealous.'

Oh. Although relieved, Nigel wasn't sure he wanted to be Patrick's confidant.

'I was staying at this awful hotel, jacked in my teaching, trying to be a writer. Trying to be! She'd definitely given me the heave-ho, all too much, think of the kids, et cetera, et cetera. I knew I'd win in the end, mind.'

Nigel sipped, concentrating on his mug. With the children, they told you not to reward negative behaviour with attention. It might work.

'There was this maid, with the—Why not, I thought? And of course the sheer mention . . . She was green. Absolutely couldn't take it, the thought of me and other women. So it was all back on from then. A sprat to catch a mackerel.' Patrick grinned wolfishly. His large teeth were an appalling sepia. 'Most enjoyable, mind.'

Yes. It was obvious cause for celebration that his mother, a married woman with two children, had been crucially provoked into abandoning them all by the fact of Patrick, a childless bachelor, fucking around. And why not revisit those carnal delights that had reunited them while he was at it?

Nigel intervened with the offer of another coffee. But from the way Patrick settled back with a cigarette as Nigel filled the kettle, he feared that they were in for the long haul. Exhaling, Patrick squared the cigarette packet, crossed his legs and cosied the chair next to his with an outstretched arm. The pose was very much Man of the Theatre. The haircut really had taken years off him.

'Of course you're right. I'll need some help.'

That was something.

'The girl's offered. Mia.' Although his inflection on the name was sarcastic, it prodded Nigel electrically. 'Putting my house in order.'

'The house . . . but surely that's not her—area of expertise . . .'

'My work. She'll help me with my work.'

Nigel spooned coffee into their recycled mugs.

'Are you sure it's a good idea? I was thinking more—a housekeeper sort of thing. Not to live in or anything, just to sort you out until you've had time to think of the future.'

'She'll sort me out, for the time being. She has the summer vacation.'

This was very bad indeed. On the other hand, Patrick was past seventy and a girl like that . . . And she'd be here, and Nigel had ongoing reasons to visit.

'What about paying her?'

'She's offered herself for free.'

There was no doubt that Patrick was enjoying playing up the unsavoury roué implications. Nigel stirred the coffees over-thoroughly, intent on dissolving the last granules that whirlpooled creamily in the centre of each mug.

'Well, if you think it's best . . .'

Nigel put Patrick's mug in front of him. Patrick flicked ash. His hand trembled and, when he spoke, his voice.

'I'll never forgive her, you know. Leaving me like this.'

He meant Mum. Well, rampaging end-stage cancer was hardly running off with the milkman. Nigel pushed the sugar bowl his way appeasingly.

'Ashes,' said Patrick. 'Oh God.' And to Nigel's dismay, he wept. Nigel hated this, always had, the way Patrick detonated instantly into high emotion, winding you in the backdraft. Still, he made an awkward clutch at Patrick's shoulder as it jerked with the incontinent rigour of his grief. Haircut or no, with the first awful sob he had become an old man. Agonising seconds passed without abatement. Nigel patted and withdrew. There was nothing to be done. How could he possibly say anything about the house now? He, at least, would conduct himself with delicacy. All that was left to him was to stand guard by the chair as Patrick, drooling a rope of wet-crumbed spittle all the way down to the table, howled on and on, alone.

C'ham Gdns
New Year's Day, 1979

Darling -

I've written pages tonight and torn them up, they're not even fit for you. Love an appalling annihilator of prose styles.

Jesus, Sara. All you need to know is that your letter has made me happier than the happiest man alive. Which is only fitting, because before this you have also made me the most abject.

Cheque enclosed, cash it at any bank, it will cover tickets and necessaries. It's direct to King's Cross as far as I can tell. Trains are regular, no point writing times, as you don't know exactly when you'll manage to get away. Drop me a line or phone once you know, and of course I'll be there to meet you. If you can't, phone from the station and hang on and I'll be no more than half an hour. Don't talk to strangers.

I live every moment for your arrival.

I had a letter from the bursar at St Christopher's confirming the place will be free for the boy after the half-term holiday in February. I've accepted, presuming it's all ok with your sister till then.

Don't be sad, my darling. You know this is the only way and the break you make is necessary in order for us to have a life together that isn't half measures and acrimony. That's the thing. Clarity will prevail, as the best for the children as much as us. No one thrives on the piecemeal and second-rate. As my love is absolute, so must yours be. I hope you can understand this. I think you do, because your instinctive capacity to understand—to understand me, at least—is one of the things I love most about you.

Longing for you every night. I kiss the left nipple, then the right, then the left again. The Green Cross Code.

For thine is the kingdom, forever and ever,

Patrick
xxx

Then

1979

Louise had starred the entry in her Letts Wombles diary as soon as Mum had written to tell her that she and Patrick and would be coming to take her out. The pencil that came with the diary wasn't very good; its lead was too hard for the shiny pages, although the snug way it tucked into the spine, with the flat brim of its white plastic top perfectly flush with the edge of the cover, hectic with Wombles, gladdened Louise's heart every time she replaced it. She considered her diary a present from Mum, since she had used some of the Christmas money Mum had sent to buy it, and Louise felt slightly guilty about how quickly she had stopped keeping it up to date. So it was good to be using the diary as it was intended, instead of manufacturing bogus reminders such as writing 'bring baking stuff for school' three days after the claggily underbaked scones had come home in their ice-cream tub and gone straight into the bin. Feeling that the pallid grey lead didn't give the visit its due importance, let alone permanence, she went over the date—March 10—in felt-tip. It would be harder, surely, to cancel an event in actual felt-tip. There had already been a couple of cancellations: one before Christmas, when the weather was too bad for Mum and Patrick to travel all the way from London, and another after, when Patrick got the flu. Third time lucky, as Auntie B said. Since she only believed in the bad kind, Auntie B invoked luck purely as a dampener. Louise could tell she was expecting another cancellation, right up to the moment when the taxi pulled up outside. It was always disappointing to be proved wrong.

Mum spilled out first, and by the time she was busy with the fiddly catch on the low iron gate, Louise was already out of the front door and halfway down the garden path. But before she could reach her, Mum had pulled back and returned to the taxi, where Patrick appeared to be having difficulties over payment. So it was Louise who released the gate's metal spring and welcomed them in, first enveloped by the smell of Mum she hadn't smelled for months and the shape she'd left behind like a cut-out, and then, suddenly, confronted by the startling new shape and smell of Patrick.

It was the very first time they'd met. Louise felt nervous, suddenly. He wasn't smiling; he was talking to Mum about the taxi.

'—tipped the bugger, he didn't know where he was going!'

Mum waved her purse with the same hand that held the strap of her smart green handbag.

'This is Louise.'

Patrick nodded. He was an immediate, complicated fact, like weather. Louise understood at once that he'd prefer to speak to her through Mum. His own voice was as posh as anyone on television, and seemed to taint Auntie B's, so that when she offered him a cup of tea inside, she braced herself before each aitch as though facing a slightly challenging stair. They were already using cups and saucers instead of mugs; Louise had helped set the table. Patrick asked for coffee to begin with, but Louise saw Mum pull a face at him and he settled for tea. While the kettle boiled she climbed into Mum's lap. Mum pulled her hair.

'What's she been feeding you, bricks?'

Eleven was too old to be sitting on your mum's knee, but it was a special occasion, after all.

'This looks nice,' Mum said, tipping her off to hover at the table. Louise had forgotten that already, the way she'd never sit in a chair. Auntie B said she had a round bum, which in fact she hadn't, but it meant she couldn't be still. 'You shouldn't have bothered, B.'

B planted the teapot.

'It's only a few biscuits. You're lucky I was off. Matron's gone sick and they've had me working all hours. Doing her job as well as everyone else's, as usual.'

'B's the brains of the family.'

Louise had grown up with the flaunting of Auntie B's brains. Nigel was assumed to take after her, although obviously boys couldn't become nurses. Patrick didn't seem particularly interested, although Mum always talked about B's brains as the end of a conversation instead of a beginning. It wasn't until they'd finished their tea and biscuits—Louise was the only one who had a biscuit, because they didn't want to spoil their lunch—and were walking to the Berni Inn that Patrick became even slightly animated. Unfortunately, it was about the Berni Inn.

'Not this prefab Merrie Englande bollocks. Can't we go somewhere where you can get a decent pint? Or even wine?'

B looked flummoxed. The Berni was the only place they ever went as a treat.

'You can get wine at a Berni,' Mum said.

'It used to be the Red Lion,' B offered.

'I'm sure it did.'

At the table, Louise watched Patrick remember to offer B a cigarette before he put the packet away (Mum didn't smoke). He wasn't her dad, but he put his penis in Mum's vagina. Every night, if Nigel's information was to be believed. Of course Nigel didn't say penis and vagina—that was from school, where they had recently been shown a film about periods ('menstruation', pronounced with eccentric emphasis on the 'u'). The boys had been removed to the gym while the screening took place, and afterwards, Louise and her friends had tantalised them with wild elaborations and exaggerations and downright lies about the censored material. But Louise knew, unlike her friends, that any or all of the improbable facts imparted about adult sexual behaviour had to be true. This weirdness must all take place, because why else would Mum leave Dad, and them? Since nothing made sense, you had to believe in a compulsion you couldn't understand. It was all because Mum wanted Patrick's penis in her vagina. Dad's penis wasn't good enough, for some reason. There were sizes, apparently. Louise had started to ask Nidge about this before he'd gone away to school, but he'd told her that she was too young to be asking those sorts of questions.

'Can I help you?'

It was the first thing Patrick had said directly to her. Mum told her to stop staring at him, and stroked his hair back from his face, smiling. She had never done this with Dad, not least because Dad's hair was much shorter. Patrick's was really quite long for his age. Not as long as a hippy, but not as short as a proper dad's.

According to the film at school, it was all to do with sperm and eggs.

'Are you going to have a baby?'

Louise wasn't saying this to Patrick in particular, but because Mum had turned back to B, who was deep in telling her something to do with Nanna and Grandpa, their mum and dad, he was the only one who caught it. He pulled back, as though the question had hit him in the face.

'I shouldn't think so.' He bared his teeth. 'Revolting things, aren't they, babies?'

It was meant to be a joke, a joke against her. He'd decided, because she was a girl, that she must love babies, and it was more a way of teasing her for that than anything else. But Louise didn't like babies. Still, she shook her head, because that was what Patrick wanted. She could tell he wasn't interested in what she really thought, and she had decided that it was best to give him what he wanted.

Patrick's face lit into a proper smile as the waiter arrived with his round tray crammed with drinks. Once they were distributed, Mum hoisted her glass of wine for a toast, although Patrick had already taken a gulp of his. She shook back her hair and stretched her neck, as though she was waiting for a photo to be taken.

'Cheers. And to Nidge, eh?'

Louise could tell Mum was wishing it was Nidge who was there instead of her. Patrick finished his drink so quickly that it was like a party trick. He reached for the bottle. He hadn't joined in the toast.

OF ALL THE new things Nigel had feared and imagined he might have to do at boarding school—Latin, rugby, fox hunting, wanking off an older boy, watching foreign films—sewing had never occurred to him. Sewing. But here he was, and Patrick was paying for it—Nigel knew exactly how much, £550 a term, because he'd secretly read the letter—sitting in the art room, expected to cross-stitch a pencil case. Even at primary this hadn't been required of him.

'It can be practical or decorative,' said the art master, Mr Hinton. 'Just do what you like, incorporating your name.'

There was an immediate bundle into the heap of felt on each table as the boys made their selection, a few tussles, good-naturedly resolved. They were thirteen, for God's sake. Nigel sat and watched, empty-handed. If only he could stop farting.

'All right Nidge, need a bit of help to get going?'

Mr Hinton, rusty-bearded, tank-topped, touched his shoulder. He showed no reaction to the fart, although the stench was unignorable. Miserably, Nigel shook his head and picked up a needle.

'Best thing is to outline the design so that you've got something to follow. Unless you're like Toby—pretty confident there, Tobe!'

Toby, who was hugely tall and had the pinkest cheeks Nigel had ever seen, beamed, pulling on a length of banana-yellow embroidery thread. Like all the boys except Nigel, his hair hung shaggily over his face and ears. Mum had ensured that Nigel had been smartly barbered before his departure, mistakenly assuming, like him, that quasi-military standards of grooming would be the norm at a school you had to pay for.

Mr Hinton patted Nigel's shoulder and moved on. 'Good chap.'

There was no choice. Cautiously letting another one go, Nigel reached for the depleted pile of felt. He chose the darkest colour, a bottle green that was the same colour as his old school blazer. There weren't even uniforms here; Patrick had thought this was a good thing.

'Soz.'

At the end of his stitch, Toby had caught the side of Nigel's head with his needle-bearing hand, which required a lot of space for its full extension. Nigel edged his chair away. Glancing at the boys around him, he folded the square of green felt into a rectangle, took up a pen and printed N I G E L. The letters sloped down to one corner, erratically spaced and pathetically small. He didn't think he could bear another forty minutes of this.

He put up his hand. 'Toilet sir.'

Mr Hinton nodded and smiled. Nigel escaped. On recent experience he could take up a good fifteen minutes in the bogs without having to eke it out. And after art there would be Latin, which he was already looking forward to. Any respite from expressing himself was already very welcome. They were big on expressing themselves at St Kit's, as they called it. In words, through the medium of embroidery thread, or even, accompanied by piano music on a reel-to-reel tape recorder and despite the fact of puberty, in movement to music. Even from the little he knew about Patrick, his choice of school astounded Nigel. His dad, without knowing any details, had been very cowed by the opportunity. That's what he'd called it, 'A big opportunity for you, son.' Mum had agreed, seizing on the same word. To her, it was a 'wonderful opportunity'. And so it had all been agreed. If his dad had known about the sewing, he would have laughed himself silly. Nigel wasn't about to write and tell him. It felt wrong to write anything at all from a place like this, like the worst sort of boasting, even if he was miserable.

The toilets were wonderfully empty. No one to ask how he was; even though all he ever said was 'fine', they kept on asking him. Nigel dropped on to the sturdy wooden seat and let it all go. He felt as though he could never get rid of all the shit there was in him. Might he have some kind of disease? Matron was supposed to deal with 'aches and pains', as she'd told him when he arrived, along with inviting him to call her Linda. She was the Head's wife's younger sister, bosomy and red-haired, and although she wasn't pretty, all of the boys made appallingly crude jokes about her that longed for her in every kind of way. It would be impossible to have a conversation with Linda about his bowels, and it wasn't as though he could write to Mum about it. He was completely on his own.

Nearly spent, Nigel rode the final cramps. They had become familiar enough over the past days that he knew they would pass. It was the porridge that had done it. He would try to avoid it from now on. Bracing his hand on the cubicle wall, he waited it out. At a concluding spasm, his nails twitched over the whitewashed brick and produced a frisson, like scratching a blackboard, that shivered him all the way up to his ears. It was repulsive. Divine. It overcame the turmoil in his arse. Taking a breath, he reached up and scored his hand down the satiny wall, in ecstasy and horror.

'Nigel?'

It was a boy, outside the cubicle. He knocked politely on the door.

'Bilbo sent me to see if you're okay.'

Bilbo, as in Baggins, as in the Hobbit, was Mr Hinton's nickname, which the teacher himself celebrated, cheerfully referring to himself as such. The huge desert-booted feet visible in the gap under the cubicle door identified his emissary as Toby.

'I'm fine.'

Nigel rattled out a length of the medicinal-smelling, waxy toilet paper from the wooden holder. Toby's feet remained planted.

'I'll be there in a minute.'

The feet retreated, but the sounds from the other side of the door suggested that Toby was determined to hang around. Perhaps he had finished his pencil case already. When Nigel pulled the chain and opened the door, Toby grinned at him from where he perched perilously on the rim of the large mesh bin next to the basins, rocking experimentally and testing his balance by lifting his feet, then stopping himself at the last possible moment from falling back into the rubbish.

'Christ, pongo,' he remarked amiably, watching Nigel wash his hands. 'Got the squits?'

Nigel said nothing. He knew that if he did, Toby would mimic it in a tin-eared version of a Yorkshire accent that sounded nothing like Nigel but gave Toby vast, unmalicious delight.

'You should go to Matron,' he advised, as Nigel tersely detached a paper towel from the holder. 'She's got all the potions. Get her to rub your face in her tits while you're at it.'

Leering, Toby forgot to check his angle and caved down into the teetering bin, which tipped to the floor with Toby in it, his rump jammed.

'Shit!'

He held his arm out for Nigel to pull him free. As Toby unselfconsciously grasped Nigel's wet, washed hand with his hot, enormous paw, the shock of being touched hit him, worse than if Toby had kicked him in the nuts. Toby's skin was surprisingly soft, the contact dismally lovely after so many physically isolated weeks. The last time Nigel had been touched was by Mum, her kiss at the station as she saw him on to the train, a hug that pushed him away more than it drew him in, bracing him for his new life. They had barely dared look at each other, because sharing what each knew of the other's feelings was worse than saying goodbye. The new life. No touching. No Louise, whose embrace had been dogged and tear-stained. The very last contact had been Patrick's brief, ambassadorial handshake.

As Toby staggered to his feet the bell rang—not an electronic bell, but a brass hand bell, serenely deployed by Guy, a retired teacher actually called Mr Fawkes, who also took on gardening duties. Nigel palmed his hand dry on his trouser leg and righted the bin, reinstating some of its scattered contents.

'You tool,' said Nigel. Out in the corridor, the smell of lunch being prepared hit him, brackish with vegetables. Already, his guts were cranking up to their next expulsion.

'Oo's tha callin' a tool, ee bah gum,' Toby said, trudging after him. A paper towel had stuck to the crepe sole of his desert boot. As Toby stopped to detach it by trampling it free with his other foot, Nigel left him behind and escaped to Latin.

BY THE TIME they were on pudding, Auntie B and Patrick were both more talkative. The two of them weren't exactly having a conversation, but no one seemed to mind. Mum sat in the middle, talking to each as they needed and chatting to Louise at the same time, with Patrick's hand on her thigh.

'It's never!'

Auntie B nudged Mum hard in the side, nodding over at a man who had come into the restaurant with his wife.

'Micky thingy! Coulter!'

'Oh my God.' Although Mum continued to smile her new smile, Louise could see she wasn't pleased.

'Aren't you going to say hello?'

Auntie B waved without waiting for Mum's answer, which would clearly have been no. It was because she didn't usually drink; she would never have waved to someone like that otherwise.

'An old flame,' B told Patrick, pulling a face.

'Brenda!' Mum tried to pull her back, but it was too late. Micky and his wife were coming over. Micky wore tight jeans and boots with a heel, but he was still smaller than his wife, who was what Louise's dad called a dollybird. She was wearing a fun-fur jacket with her jeans, which were as tight as Micky's but looked far better on her.

'Christ on a bike,' Patrick said, before they reached them.

'You bitch, B,' said Mum, without disturbing her smile of welcome.

Micky seemed truly delighted to see Mum and Auntie B, but most of all to see Mum. His wife and Patrick were undelighted as he exclaimed, 'Look at you!' and gave Mum a wet kiss, moving on to B with more politeness and less enthusiasm. They didn't talk for long, since it was clear no one had much to say to each other. Micky was doing building contracting, and he and his wife, who had been at school with Mum and B and was called Janet, had three boys. They were celebrating Janet's birthday. Janet said it was pricey at the Berni but always worth it, and anyway, Micky was paying. She took a long, curious look at Patrick while they were all talking, but he remained unintroduced. Then she raked an even more curious look over Mum's clothes, which were unlike anything else being worn in the room, and protectively stroked her fun fur.

'Could have been you,' said B, as Micky and Janet moved off to their table. Mum picked up her wine glass.

'I don't think so.'

B leaned over her to Patrick. At some point during the meal she seemed to have become more interested in him than she was in Mum.

'He played the guitar. Mum and Dad hated that, their daughter going off with a pop star—they thought it was the end of the world!'

'We were kids,' Mum protested.

'You were mad about him! Used to sneak out and all sorts!'

'What was I supposed to do? They stopped me seeing him.'

Patrick kissed Mum on the ear. 'Would you like me to challenge him to a duel?'

He was joking.

Mum leaned into him. 'Go on then,' she said, as Patrick moved his lips through her hair, smiling.

B dropped back against her chair cushion. Louise could see her disappointment. Something hadn't worked. Things tended not to, for Auntie B.

'You always had to be different,' she said, to Mum, but for Patrick.

'Me?'

'She did! Always. Nothing were ever good enough. Princess and the bloody pea we used to call her at home.'

Mum made the closed-mouth bark that pretended to be laughter when something wasn't funny. She never said much, but when she was angry she stopped talking altogether. She shook her hair out again and did the stretching thing with her neck. Squeezing her hand, Patrick called the waiter and ordered another bottle of wine.

'But we've had our pudding,' said Auntie B. She looked shocked, although the waiter didn't. Mum made another bark and B wheeled to look at her, a fight ready in her face, but Patrick was too quick for her.

'Brenda my love, if you won't have another drink, the rest of the world will have to have it for you.'

And incredibly, Patrick picked up B's hand and kissed it, so that B blushed and called him a daft bugger. He had won, just like that—Louise didn't understand how. But Mum laughed, and Patrick kissed her, laughing himself for some reason, so that his mouth laughed against her laughter. Louise wished she could kiss Mum too, but there was no room. The waiter delivered the wine and Auntie B had some after all. Louise's Coke was long drained, and she resorted to dry slurps of the straw. Still, everyone was happy now. Mum was happy. That was what Patrick could do.

Part Two

SARA sits on the outcrop. It's starting to get dark. Sound of the sea beyond, behind her. She ignores the sea and looks straight out to the audience. She's on the lookout for someone. Alert. NASH and GIL cross from SR, both smoking. They're in uniform.

GIL: You waiting for someone, love?

SARA nods.

NASH: Sure it's not us?

GIL: When's it ever us, Nash boy?

NASH: Show us your tits.

Impassively, and still on the lookout, SARA pulls off the top part of her gown, revealing her bare breasts. NASH and GIL don't see this, as they've walked DS.

NASH: Farting in the wind.

GIL: Speak for yourself.

NASH: The lot of them. Farting in the wind.

GIL: Pissing in the wind, isn't it?

NASH: Fuck off.

GIL: Pissing in the wind, whistling in the dark.

NASH: Farting in the wind.

GIL: Shitting their kegs.

NASH: Fuck off. The lot of them, is what I'm saying.

GIL: We'll all be shitting our kegs come tomorrow, Nashy boy.

NASH: Fuck off.

GIL: The lot of us. Them and all.

GIL and NASH turn back. They see SARA.

GIL: You slag.

NASH: Sure you're waiting for someone, love?

SARA: He's late.

GIL: Pull the other one—it's got bells on.

NASH: Mine hasn't.

SARA: I'm waiting for the colonel. Do you know him?

GIL: Oh, we know the colonel all right, don't we, Nash boy?

NASH: We know the colonel like the back of our hands.

SARA: With bells on?

NASH offers SARA a cigarette from his packet. She declines it.

NASH: Go on, it's good for your health.

SARA shakes her head.

NASH: Save it for later then.

He takes the cigarette and places it behind her ear. SARA takes it and offers it back to him.

SARA: It's a waste.

GIL: Give it to the colonel. He likes a smoke, doesn't he, Nash boy?

NASH: Not half. Fag-ash Lil, the colonel.

SARA replaces the cigarette behind her ear.

NASH: Do I get a little kiss?

GIL: For the snout?

NASH: Just a peck on the cheek.

SARA takes the cigarette and again offers it back to NASH.

SARA: I think the colonel smokes a different brand.

NASH doesn't take the cigarette. SARA drops it to the ground.

NASH: Got it first time, Gil; she's a slag.

GIL: Right little slapper, anyone can see that.

NASH: Tits hanging out for the world to see.

GIL: Flashing her lilies.

NASH: How much does the colonel pay you, love?

SARA: How much does he pay you?

NASH and GIL move in. GIL holds SARA as NASH rapes her. SARA doesn't resist, but as the attack escalates, her cry pierces the air.

SARA: England!!!

END OF ACT 1

(From *Bloody Empire*, 1982)

Now

AUTUMN

THE MAGAZINE page had dropped from the pristine flyleaf of an unused recipe book. The book was part of a sparse collection that all looked, from the honeyed glazes and maraschino garnishes of the shots on their covers, to have been acquired at the same time—the 1980s—and never looked at. Sara was no cook. Mia would have known that from the state of the kitchen, even if Patrick didn't often make the point himself when she served him a meal. Sometimes it was announced as a compliment, as he took the first approving bite, or as exculpation, when his palate faltered at an unfamiliar, and to his mind exotic, dish. That was his age, not Mia's cooking. She was a really good cook. It was what she'd enjoyed most about the summer weeks, having the run of the clapped-out kitchen.

Mia shook the spine, expecting to release the article's facing page, but all that resulted was the protesting crackle of elderly glue. Her fingers slipped along the sleek, still inky-smelling pages of Chicken Marengo and Spanish Puffs. Empty; this was all there was. Most of the magazine fragment was taken up by half a picture. Looking at it, Mia recognised young versions of Patrick and Sara. There was more of him than of her, their dark bodies invaded by white text.

'He Doesn't Even Like Me To Say the B-Word!'
Woman's Own meets controversial playwright
Patrick Conway and his wife, Sa
their rugged Cornish retreat.

Mia replaced the page in the flyleaf, setting the book on the pile already taken from the shelf. Along with the others she had removed, the book's negative was visible on the grimy wall behind. This reminded her about chasing up the last lot of painters for a quote: she already had two stored in her mobile, and it would be good to make a start.

The third painter never seemed to answer his phone. Mia decided not to leave another message. As she waited for the Yell app to buffer so that she could go about finding someone else, Mia retrieved the magazine page and chucked it in the bin. *So much crap.*

It was interesting though. Overall. Mia reminded herself of this whenever Patrick went on about things she found boring, or repeated himself; that to someone on the outside, her situation was very interesting indeed. Through July and August she had enjoyed imagining people on her course reading the artfully casual update she'd put on Facebook: '*She's got an internship with this old writer, he has this amazing house in Cornwall?*' For maximum impact, they'd have to know who Patrick was. Or at least they should know that Patrick had been famous, back in the day, if not properly, then at least famous enough to know some really famous people, the kind who were quoted and whose deaths got announced everywhere. It was old school, but Mia didn't care. She was so used to being different, she not only liked it, she sought it out. For example, the way she dressed: only people who knew could see the quality of what she wore, so lengthily saved for, her boots shined. It made her a different kind of person, just as her dad had always told her. *Don't run with the crowd, babe.* The point was, being here would look amazing on her CV, burnished into 'PA to playwright Patrick Conway'.

CV apart, though, it was getting harder to deny that money was on the verge of becoming an issue. After Patrick had invited her to stay for the vacation, Mia had given notice on her flat-share back in Newcastle and cleared out all her stuff. She didn't have the cash to keep the rent up all through the summer without a serious job, and the 'board' Patrick was offering her turned out to mean little more than a roof over her head. It had panicked her a little, putting her belongings into store, although she didn't want to renew the tenancy on the flat, which was a rip-off, miles from the town centre and freezing in the winter, with tiny, gloomy rooms. Besides, she'd have had to find flatmates to replace the two Italian girls she'd been sharing with, who had gone back to Turin at the end of term. It was beyond irritating, interviewing people you had no interest in even talking to but had to evolve a kind of intimacy with, however much you lived your own life; their unflushed crap in the toilet. Never again, she'd vowed, not if she could help it.

Patrick himself wasn't an entirely reliable flusher, but he was old. So was his toilet, for that matter. And although he wasn't paying her anything apart from what he called housekeeping, at least he had proved flexible with the sums he doled out to her. Mia was scrupulous about giving Patrick change and receipts (which he never looked at) and the only money she held back was for things like toiletries. She could imagine Patrick calling this category 'unmentionables'. He could be quite funny, in his way. Mia had been truly surprised to find this during their first week alone together, because, as she had told him, his play was so serious.

'Of course it's serious, my love, but it's fucking hilarious! Haven't you ever seen it?'

Obviously she hadn't. She'd actually only skip-read it on the train on the way down to see him that first time. It was hard to imagine it being funny. Mia had never really got plays, and the ones about issues, which this one clearly was, she found the most unfathomable, Shakespeare apart. She had come to *Bloody Empire* purely because her dissertation subject, controversy as media commodity (her supervisor Jonathon's suggestion), needed a period that was academically uncolonised. Mia's idle googling had turned serious as she had begun to realise that the Falklands War, which had taken place eight years before she was born, almost certainly had a dissertation in it. She knew that Jonathon would object if he could, so she ensured that when she suggested 'Conflict (re)solutions: media controversies in representations of the Falklands crisis, 1982', she was confident it hadn't already been done. Since their thing, Jonathon had become very severe, overcorrecting the bias that had led to their thing in the first place. It was all a bit late in the day, in Mia's opinion. And although she definitely wasn't going to make that mistake again, she doubted very much that she could say the same for Jonathon. She had seen him leching over that fat-arsed girl with the piercings in their seminar group. So needy.

Outside the kitchen, Mia's phone finally flagged up a sturdy little xylophone of reception; there was no rhyme or reason to the coverage in the house, you just had to take the opportunity. Proceeding alphabetically, she rejected the firm called Abel Decorators because she knew Patrick would make a comment about the name, as though she hadn't noticed. She settled for Atkinson Home Décor, who answered promptly and sounded professional. 'Décor' was itself hardly a Patrick-friendly word, but she would just refer to them as Atkinson's if they came back with a competitive quote.

It was funny, now that she knew him well enough to second-guess his prejudices, to think that only a few months ago Patrick had been no more than a couple of prospective footnotes. The email that Sara had replied to so scrupulously had been one of ten Mia had composed to possible key sources. Three of her authors, she later discovered, had been dead for some years, one had Alzheimer's and, of the rest, only Sara had been so quickly responsive. Mia was pleased by the imagined cachet of citing a conversation with a living author, however forgotten, in her dissertation. It was classy and attention-grabbing. It showed the kind of flair she could talk up in interviews as evidence of journalistic instincts, bound to impress. *Don't run with the crowd, babe.*

So Mia had replied promptly and enthusiastically to Sara's email, which was formally composed, like a letter, with occasional, surprising spelling errors that might have been due to a lack of keyboard skills. The chance of meeting an actual person was far more appealing than spending any more time in the over-lit faculty library, or surfing her laptop in some sticky-tabled café. When she had rocked up to discover that Sara had died, she was forced to roll with the punches. But she was good at that, she had discovered.

Only her excellent plan to wrap up her dissertation while performing her minimal duties for Patrick hadn't quite worked, in that it was now almost the end of September, and she still had about a quarter of the writing to go before term began. Mia was annoyed with herself about this lapse in efficiency, although it was something she had encountered before, when the making of meticulous schedules for undergraduate assessments had, it transpired, taken the place of actual work, and she had come close to failing more than one of the modules. (Thank God Jonathon had put in a good word about her MA application.) During her time in Cornwall she had made a point of applying herself regularly to her dissertation, but despite scrolling through the document, tweaking its formatting and amplifying its footnotes and bibliography, she failed to inch much towards the full ten thousand words. She couldn't really blame Patrick for that, talkative as he could be. His family—the stepdaughter and stepson—had left them alone, although the stepson had announced the need for a 'family summit' when he returned from his summer holiday in Puglia. The washing and cooking and shopping didn't fill much of the day. It was the house, and her plans for the house, that consumed her.

Mia's obsession with houses had bloomed when she started secondary, coincident with realising that she couldn't bring any of her new friends back to the humiliating Barratt box she and Mum had ended up in after her parents split. The teenage Mia had read *Wallpaper** the way other girls read *Heat*. She had even had a declared period of wanting to be an architect before she discovered how much maths was involved, and her closest sixth-form friendship, with a girl called Jessica Norton, had been founded on discovering that she lived in a staggering Georgian terrace her parents had had gutted at the back and transformed by a brutalist extension featured in several interiors magazines. Jessica herself had been elusively silent, masking dullness, but that suited Mia, who herself preferred quiet. She had happy memories of the mute afternoons the two of them spent together, sprawled on the Italian modular sofa pretending to do homework, feet warmed on the underfloor heating, skin flattered by concealed lighting. At any moment she had felt they were worthy of an advertorial magazine spread.

Although Patrick's house was the squalid opposite of Jessica's, from the first time Mia saw it, fully expecting to meet Sara, she had been stirred by the potential amid the ruin. There was just so much of it, all original features: it was one big Before, waiting for her to turn it into a stripped-down, reglazed After. In the summer weeks, instead of analysing the examples she had chosen of the primitive media's appropriations of the Falklands War, she had been clearing and rearranging, carrying out the smallest portion of the renovations and improvements she was undertaking in her head. Now though, she had to admit to herself that her time was running out. Term was about to start and she would be homeless in ten days. She'd done nothing about finding another flat, not so much as checked out a property website: from so far away, it was frankly quite hard even to believe in Newcastle. Staring at the block of dissertation text on her laptop screen, Mia deplored her increasingly unignorable provisionality. She had thought that she was following a plan. *Always have a plan, babe. Plan A, and plan B.* Thanks, Dad.

Tipping onion skins into the kitchen bin—she was making shepherd's pie, since the stir-fry she had produced the previous night had 'nearly taken the roof of my fucking mouth off,' according to Patrick—the youthful fragments of him and Sara enticed her. She retrieved the brittle magazine page. Sara was visible only as a section of waving gold-brown hair and a slender hand brushing Patrick's denim-shirted shoulder. He occupied most of the shot, his own hair black, as it still was only in the photos around the house. His expression though, was untouched by time. *Uncompromising.*

The pinging of her email startled Mia away from the bin. Expecting the quote promised by Atkinson Home Décor, she leaned over to her open laptop, resting on the stack of discardable recipe books, to retrieve the new mail. Sure enough, and pleasingly, the quote Atkinson's had come in with was the lowest of the three she had sought. Jotting it down, Mia scrolled past several junk messages that were part of the most recent haul and halted at the last message. It was from Jonathon, using his sober university email address.

Subject: Dissertation

Hi Mia,

Hope you've had a good summer. Can you confirm a tutorial meeting to discuss the progress of your dissertation on Monday October 8th at 9.30 in my office? As you may know, the restructuring of the undergraduate degree course has meant my workload has increased dramatically over the last academic year in terms of the modules I'm both teaching and marking. Consequently, I've spoken to Harbinder Singh, lecturer in communications, who has agreed to take over supervision for you and some of my other MA students. As you know, Harbinder's an excellent tutor and very excited at the prospect of being on board with your work, which is in her field. I've copied her into this email, as she'll also be at the meeting on the 8th.

Please let me know you can attend as soon as possible, in case we need to rearrange an alternative time for that week.

I look forward to hearing from you,
Jonathon

Mia clammed the lid of her laptop. *Some other of my MA students. Harbinder Singh.* It wasn't as though she'd had feelings for Jonathon, but his lack of flair was painful. She should never have ignored the warning of the 'Keep Calm and Carry On' poster the first time she went to his flat, instead of deluding herself because of his Missoni scarf, which turned out to have been a present from a tasteful ex-girlfriend. *As you know.* Jonathon had a nervous habit of folding things—napkins, receipts, seminar notes, takeaway menus—as he spoke to you, drawing attention to the tapering deftness of his fingers as he drew them along the edge of the crease as precisely as origami. She'd noticed this at the beginning; along with the scarf, it had seemed to promise delicacy, a discerning capacity for attention. In fact, it was just a random nervous habit.

Keep Calm and Carry On. What the fuck was she going to do?

It was so unfair, the way some people were just given things. Jessica lived in Thailand now, a remote if aggravating Facebook friend. Her parents had sold the house and opened a resort hotel outside Phuket. Mia had never yet received an invitation solid enough to convert into a visit.

With unnecessary concentration, Mia spooned a perfect, crusted mound of shepherd's pie on to the exact centre of Patrick's warmed plate and carried the tray into his study, which was where he preferred to eat. Handing him his cutlery as she balanced the tray on one spread palm, she announced her progress in nailing down the best quote for repainting the kitchen.

'I'll make sure I've got paper quotes, though,' Mia reassured him. 'I don't think any of them will be able to start before the week after next and I'll be gone by then, but as long as you've got it in writing, they'll have to stick to it.'

Patrick grunted assent as Mia leant to slide the tray down in front of him. As she always did at this moment, Mia ignored his canine alertness to her breasts and glanced past him through the window into the garden. It was a beautiful evening, full of opaque, eliding Cornish greys and greens and creams, the scrap of sea as lively as an eye. She had Instagrammed this very view shortly after arriving. Talking to Patrick about the painting work made the thought of not being there in the house to see what only she cared about even more desperate: 8 October loomed. Harbinder Singh loved an argument and, despite being a lesbian, had had no time at all for Mia when she had taken, and got that bare pass in, her undergraduate Feminism and Film module.

Below her eyeline, Patrick mouthed his shepherd's pie. Silence from him always meant enjoyment. *Keep Calm.* Still intent on the garden, Mia tussled with the miniature button below the collar of her blouse, which was rather stiff (usually, she pulled the teasingly prim garment on and off over her head without troubling herself with its fastenings). The buttons were heart-shaped, a little retro. Releasing the next button exposed the bruise-coloured lace of her excellent bra. Rigby & Peller. They rarely had sales, but it was worth waiting. And they fitted you properly: she had surprisingly full breasts for her narrow back.

Without looking down, Mia could feel Patrick relax; less aroused, apparently, than relieved.

'Might I?'

His tone was unusually humble, less optimistic of her gratifying his request than of her fetching ketchup for his shepherd's pie.

'No,' Mia told him, still relishing the view. In her experience, knowing what you wanted was half the battle. As her dad said, it sorted the men from the boys. *Plan A, and plan B.* Leaving the button as it was, she went to get the ketchup.

From the *Daily Telegraph*

Letter to the Editor
April 12, 1982

Sir,

While I pride myself on a certain acumen, and certainly subscribe to a view of history as the account of mankind's doom to ignorant repetition, I would have to be nothing short of psychic to have written 'a clumsily abstract and frequently obscene leftist attack on the Falklands conflict'. My play had its first performance at the National Theatre on April 9th, a week after the first shots were exchanged in the South Atlantic. Does your critic have any idea of how a play is written, rehearsed and produced?

Yours,
Patrick Conway
Author, 'Bloody Empire'
Cobham Gardens
London N8

From *The Times*

Letter to the Editor
May 2, 1982

Sir,

Your correspondent E. Jarrett (Letters, April 30th) may be interested to know that I have never been a member of the Communist Party, nor of the Socialist Workers Party, Labour Party, Conservatives, Liberals or any other political party. I do not join parties. As my wife will corroborate, I seldom even attend them.

Respectfully,
P. Conway
Author, 'Bloody Empire'
London N8

OBVIOUSLY, MIA KNEW Nigel wanted to have sex with her; men did. Men in shops, boys at uni, Jonathon, blokes in clubs, friends' dads. But she could tell that he wasn't the kind of man to make it a problem, so when Patrick grumbled about Nigel wanting to pay another visit, she realised he must have some reason more compelling than her. He was a kind of lawyer—trademarks, apparently, although she only knew that from googling. Patrick had no idea what he really did, because he had no interest in Nigel. The firm's website, as much as Nigel's demeanour and the clothes he wore, confirmed to Mia that he was worth keeping on side. She suspected that this visit might have something to do with the legal documents she had found in Patrick's desk, still folded and unexamined—documents to do with the house, from what she understood, as well as others concerning his play.

'Does he want to stay here? I can get a room ready.'

Patrick snorted and said they weren't a bloody hotel. In any case, Nigel was going to bring his family down with him, and he wouldn't take the bloody liberty. Mia was a little deflated to hear this; she would have enjoyed the preparations. One of her current reveries was in fact the conversion of the house into a boutique hotel. They could offer seven large bedrooms, perhaps centred around a theatrical theme, given Patrick's background. Shakespeare was obviously naff, and geographically wrong. Maybe themes were naff in themselves, as at weddings? In any case, there would have to be bathrooms installed. She had had to park the idea for now, but it was definitely one for the future.

In the weeks since the deadline for Mia's return to Newcastle had passed, Jonathon had sent an escalating run of emails, wondering what had happened to her. Mia hadn't replied to any of them. Responding to the one missed call from him on her mobile (no message, typically craven), Mia had simply texted: 'Not returning. Will msg. Mia.' She hadn't messaged. There had been another missed call, then a bewildered but still official email in which Jonathon had included the email address of the university counselling service and cc'd both the chief counsellor and the head of humanities. Since then, Mia had severed her ties with the university by way of actual, printed-out letters, none of them addressed to Jonathon.

Throughout this time Patrick looked, but he neither touched nor asked to.

'My cock doesn't work,' he had told her, a few days into the blouse-button routine. 'Shut up shop years ago.'

It had made everything more possible. Even at its most enjoyable, sex always made Mia feel she was missing the point of something others deployed to enhance their status by claiming to find it transformational—much like those who trumpeted their love of the theatre. Well, she was different, as usual. Her pleasure was mild enough when she fancied someone, like Jonathon; it would be downright impossible with Patrick. But if she didn't want to and he was unable to, couldn't that work, for both of them? As far as Mia had observed, relationships were problematic if there were inequalities in what each party wanted: money, sex, conversation, three proper holidays a year including skiing. As hadn't been the case with her parents, she and Patrick balanced each other out. It wasn't a relationship, exactly, but given her lack of options, she was beginning to think it had nearly as much potential as the house.

Patrick's only request, when she had brought in a tray one day with her hair in a ponytail because she had been frying steak and hated the spit of fat in her hair, was for her to let her hair down. It was that day Patrick had told her about his cock not working. Otherwise they had conducted themselves as they had through the summer, talking to each other normally and watching TV together in the evenings. Mia had never watched TV like that before, as though it was a hobby. She found it quaint. Patrick conscientiously underlined likely programmes in the TV guide you got with the Sunday paper (reading newspapers was another new pastime), teeing up the week's viewing. Far from the searing documentaries and subtitled films she would have imagined, he based his schedule entirely around crime dramas and sport. He shouted at both, and ads often tipped him into overdrive. Mia had quickly learned to field the remote, particularly if the National Lottery was involved.

A couple of weeks after the beginning of the university term, while she was flicking channels one night to find something less inflammatory than the Thunderball show announcing the numbers, Patrick put his large dry hand over hers. They were sitting next to each other, knees high and bums low in the shot sofa cushions. As Mia looked at him, one hand trapped, the other aiming the remote, Patrick brought up a trembling sigh.

'Do stay, won't you?'

She said nothing, but nor did she withdraw. After a second or two, his own hand had retracted. She found the end of a *DCI Banks* and they watched it in silence, save for Patrick's outburst about an unconvincing pathologist. There was no need to speak of Patrick's offer, or the tentative pass that accompanied it; it changed nothing of their routine. Mia stayed. Still, she found herself unusually nervous at the sound of Nigel's four-by-four crunching into the drive late on the Friday afternoon he and his family were due.

Nigel immediately ran to use the bathroom, leaving Mia to greet his wife and children. There was no sign of Patrick, who had taken to his study. The small boys, introduced as Oliver and Albie, were asleep in the back of the car, heads lolled against the wings of their child seats, soft mouths agape.

'It's too bloody far!' complained Sophie. 'We tried to keep them awake. I told Nigel, we're the ones who'll suffer! They won't sleep tonight!'

Little about Nigel's wife surprised Mia, except for the fact that she was about ten years younger than Nigel, and a notch better-looking. Either Nigel was better off than she had thought, or Sophie had self-esteem issues. From the open way Sophie eyed Mia up and down before she swung into the house, wondering where Patrick was in a voice modulated to command, Mia decided it was more likely to be a money thing. Nigel himself looked uneasy as he came downstairs and saw Sophie making a beeline for Patrick's study.

'Maybe Patrick's working, Sophe?'

But it was all fine. Sophie had taken the precaution of bringing a bottle of thirty-year-old single malt as a gift for Patrick, and she was all fawning flirtatiousness, which Mia was amazed to see actually worked, a little. Mia had learned that often the worst thing you could do was try to please Patrick but, as with everything, it depended on his mood, and if you were a woman, what you looked like. Sophie was quite pretty in a bog-standard Boden way—good legs that excused a soft middle that was probably due to the kids, decent skin. That wiggy middle-aged hair, blonde of course. With people, as with houses, Mia enjoyed imaginative renovation. No woman should ever wear a rugby shirt, even with the collar up, let alone in mint green and pink, let alone with diamond stud earrings. On the other hand, Sophie already had her family, and perhaps she dressed like that to close the age gap with Nigel. Maybe Nigel even liked it?

The two of them only stayed for a cup of tea, pleading the hotel check-in, as well as the boys, still sleeping out in the car. As she presented a mug of Earl Grey to Sophie, Mia clocked the full value of the other woman's distraction, intent on the worm-drilled roof beams above her. It was the house. She was there to scope out the house for herself, the cow, while Nigel sealed the deal with Patrick in some way, using his legal magic. Mia had stayed with enough school friends in Cornwall with mothers from the same gene pool as Sophie. She was probably already picking out muted paint colours and lining up friends for half term.

'Let's hope TripAdvisor doesn't lie!' Sophie said, as Mia followed her back to the car. (Patrick hadn't been so charmed that he felt it necessary to see them out.) Nigel arranged that they would drop by after breakfast the following day. Every time he talked to Mia directly he blushed, and she could see Sophie noticing. *Awkward*. Although Sophie wasn't detained for long, her frosty-shadowed eyes intent on the porch, mentally replacing the vast corpse of creeper with wisteria.

Nigel overcame the blushing to speak to her before he got into the passenger seat. He wanted to know if Patrick had heard from Nigel's sister, Louise. Mia told him that as far as she knew, they'd heard nothing since Louise had been down for Sara's funeral. And she did know. Ringing phones—and they didn't ring very much—were one of her jobs.

'She called me when we were loading the car,' said Nigel. 'She was in a bit of a state, to be honest. But that's nothing new.'

'I can't see why she'd ring Patrick anyway, can you?'

Nigel smiled, pinking again, and agreed.

'Maybe it was a false alarm.'

But that night, while she and Patrick were watching *Scott & Bailey*, the doorbell rang. Sure enough, it was Louise, trailing her daughter behind her. Holly looked furious and Louise tremulous, verging on tears while brimming with some uncommunicated anger of her own.

'We've got to stay,' she announced, pulling Holly closer to her. 'It's an emergency.'

When Mia let them over the threshold, Louise's anger seemed to vanish, as though surrendering a weapon she'd armed herself with for an argument that hadn't materialised.

'Thank God,' she wept, as Holly rolled her eyes. Holly was definitely still angry, Mia could see. Already, and it surprised her, she missed the peace of summer. It was true what Patrick had said that morning: the hordes were descending.

From the *Guardian*

Letter to the Editor
May 10th 1982

Sir,

At the risk of biting the hand that feeds me, I take strong exception to Michael Billington's review of my play, 'Bloody Empire'. It does not 'draw outraged attention to the slaughter of young working-class men in the symbolic defence of an impotent imperialism'. That may be his view of what's happening in Port Stanley—I can assure him it's not the case at the Cottesloe. Perhaps he left before the end of Act Two?

Yours etc,
Patrick Conway
London N8

In the night, a hand touched Mia's face. Warm and soft, it left her skin and returned to it, rhythmic and loving. She was a cat being stroked, moulded by the blissful comfort the hand dispensed. There were words, nonsense words in a language she couldn't speak, but she knew their translation: *Everything's going to be all right. Everything's going to be all right. Everything—*

She woke, the hand still on her cheek and a scream in her throat.

'Sorry.' Louise hovered over her, her bulk blocking the unresolved light from the door. Mia was sleeping in the den, having sacrificed the spare room bed to Louise and Holly. 'She's gone—I don't know what to do.'

It took seconds for the words to find their edge. Louise was already sobbing, which was no good to anyone.

'Sure she's not just in the loo or something?'

But as she followed Louise out into the corridor, Mia saw that the lights leading down the hall blazed a trail to where the kitchen door stood open to the cold dark. Weaker than the electric glare inside, the penumbra of moon on sea still cast enough light to show the garden was empty. The drive, when Mia walked it, was also empty, and all the visible road beyond. Louise was right—Holly was gone.

She'd seemed docile enough when Louise had pitched up with her, despite her underlying mood. Once Mia had let them in, Louise had started gabbling about Holly's bad behaviour with a boyfriend and Louise's determination to get her away from him. Apparently the boyfriend was much older than Holly, although Mia suspected a racist element in Louise's disapproval—his name was Nish. Holly had been caught lying about staying out with him all night and beyond this Mia became hazy, since Louise's distress had escalated into incoherence, at which point Holly had started shouting (among other things) that her mother didn't know what she was talking about. It seemed that Louise thought the boyfriend had attacked Holly, but this was possibly just Louise's way of accounting for the sexual contact, which Mia could see was borderline unsuitable, given the girl's age. What was she, barely fourteen? Certainly Holly wanted to be with this boy, whatever he was supposed to have done, but she also seemed twitchy and blenched to a degree unwarranted by just having a row with her mum, even if Louise did appear unhinged. Not least because, in her blind impulse to remove Holly from the boyfriend's sphere of influence, she'd thrown herself on Patrick's mercy.

'You must be a fucking lunatic, coming here.' Behind Patrick's forceful delivery, his face betrayed an elderly faltering at the female distress invading his world.

Mia had sent him to bed, telling him she'd deal with it and it would all be sorted out in the morning. Once he'd gone, Louise calmed a little and Mia managed to hustle mother and daughter into the spare room, dissipating the turmoil with cups of tea and the search for clean sheets. It was pleasing to discover that she was good in someone else's crisis, even someone she found as annoying as Louise, and actually, now their peace had been breached, doing something after so many weeks of lassitude was oddly enjoyable.

Now, though, there was this—more crises to come. Louise shuddered in the kitchen, fighting for breath.

'She's took my phone.'

Louise had confiscated Holly's own mobile back in Leeds. Obviously she needed a way to stay in contact with the boyfriend and had filched the phone from her mother's bag, along with some cash. After making Louise sit down, Mia headed for the hall phone to ring the police. It also occurred to her to ring Nigel.

Mia had never had cause to call out the police before; once they arrived, they made her feel unaccountably uneasy. Patrick, roused by the comings and goings while on one of his customary nighttime forays for a pee, declared them a useless fucking waste of time. Louise gabbled her story indiscriminately at both the woman officer and Mia, although the WPC was the only one with a notebook. Not that she wrote much in it, Mia observed. The male officer stayed outside on the drive, nudging conversationally into the radio strapped up near his neck and keeping a redundant eye on their patrol car. There was no sense of urgency, except from Louise, who was hoping the police might intercept Holly at the train station, although the twenty pounds Holly had filched from her purse was hardly enough for the train fare all the way back to Leeds, even on a child ticket. Louise was convinced Leeds was where she was headed, to get back to her boyfriend, if boyfriend was the right word. 'Older', from the account Louise had given the police, turned out to be closer to thirty than twenty. For the first time since she had arrived, Mia felt sympathetic to Louise's distress. When Mia first arrived at Patrick's after Sara's funeral, she had more than once seen Holly sucking her thumb as she watched TV, her eye-rolling pose of disaffection slackened into infancy once she stopped watching herself pretend to be an adult.

'She can't bloody stay away from him,' Louise sobbed, as though she hadn't already been through all this with Mia and Patrick earlier in the evening. The WPC reassured her, for the fourth or fifth time, that there was no train for Holly to board until the earliest one left towards six. Her colleague was speaking to one of their cars near the station—they had seen no sign of her as yet. This didn't console Louise in any way. 'Anything could happen to her,' she insisted, 'it's pitch dark out there.'

Just as Patrick announced that he was going back to bed, Nigel arrived, incongruously spruce and alert and intrusive with aftershave. By comparison the police officers seemed blurred, as though they'd been asleep themselves when they got the call. Nigel took charge, which appeared to be his thing. Mia felt a lurch of irritation; she'd been doing so well.

'Does this man have a car?' he asked. The question, which apparently hadn't occurred to the police, diverted Louise's torrent of distress into an overflow about him hanging around giving Holly lifts, Louise not knowing a thing about it until the night Holly had gone missing back home, her thinking Holly was at a school disco, getting a text from her saying she was staying with her friend Scarlett, but when she'd checked up to see they'd got back to Scarlett's safely, it was Scarlett who had told her about the lifts and presents, the way the bastard wouldn't leave her alone—

Nigel shut her up. 'Louise, if he has a car, and they haven't picked her up at the station, isn't it more likely she's arranged to meet her boyfriend out on the motorway somewhere?'

Louise clamped her hand over her mouth and did some rocking. The WPC said that they could put the word out to highway patrols, but beyond that . . . Mia allowed a yawn to swell behind her teeth until it was big enough to swallow. It was too late now to follow Patrick back to bed.

'There's really not much more we can do, at this point,' said the WPC. 'She might turn up, change her mind. You know what kids are like at that age. You say there was no argument at all?'

Louise wept. 'If I saw him, I'd kill him,' she said. 'I'd get a knife and stick it in the bastard. I would.'

'I don't think the officer needs to hear that,' said Nigel.

The copper glued to the radio appeared with the emptied mug of tea Mia had made for him, and the WPC took this as their signal to leave, promising to ring with any developments. Once they had gone, Louise degenerated into gulps and shakings. Mia wondered whether she or Nigel should slap her. Nigel seemed equally uncertain; he stood by his sister, his fingers twiddling anxious octaves at the end of his rigid arms, unsure of which note to play.

'Louise.'

She didn't respond. 'Weezer.' Nigel said it as self-consciously as a word attempted in an unpractised foreign language. 'Come on now. This isn't helping anyone.'

'Sorry.' Louise's speech was thick, waterlogged. She calmed a little.

'I'll go out in the car myself and look for her. If you think about it, he's not going to be able to get down from Leeds for hours. Unless they had an arrangement.'

'I wouldn't put it past him. I just thought, if you can get her away, get her away, Louise . . .'

Mia offered to go with Nigel. She didn't want to stay and listen to more of Louise's distress. Sitting in Nigel's Audi, as he apologised for the child seats in the back even though she was sitting in the front, she realised how long it had been since she had left the house. It was actually good to be doing something different, however bizarre.

The lanes were still dark as they criss-crossed towards the Newquay road. Mia kept watch from her window for Holly's small, square figure trudging along the verges, but all she saw were rabbits, skittering out of the headlights' beam.

'You must think we're a strange lot,' Nigel said.

Since this was unanswerable, Mia didn't. She was aware of Nigel flicking a look at her. They drove on through the empty countryside. Once they got on to the B road, there were other cars, although not many.

'What's *your* family like?' He asked this as though he was making a joke.

'Oh, well, you know . . . I've left home and everything.'

Three texts to her mum since June. There had been voice messages, asking her to call back. But she had to live her own life:

Mum was the first one to say that. Anyway, she had half been waiting until she could send some news. That's what Mum liked, that's what she always pressed her for, definite news. Progress. Well, there was news of a kind. Mia felt like testing it out on Nigel.

'This is kind of random, but Patrick wants me to stay. As a more permanent . . . as his assistant, kind of thing.'

Although there was no deviation in his steering, Mia felt the instant entirety of Nigel's tension at the wheel.

'Right,' he said after a second or two. And then, after a second or two more, 'And what about your degree?'

'It's . . . I mean, I'm happy to, for now. I've kind of put a pin in finishing my MA.'

By her side, Nigel performed a series of driverly mannerisms, checking his rear-view and side mirrors, running his hands along the top of the steering wheel and back to ten-to-two, adjusting the ventilation flap nearest to him.

'Patrick, you know . . . I think he's lonely.' Saying it, Mia realised it might even be true. A mild, unfathomable noise came from Nigel. She couldn't tell if it was emotional or digestive.

'I mean, it's kind of an amazing opportunity,' she said. 'Helping him with his writing. I've never met anyone like him.'

'No,' said Nigel. 'He's a bit of a nightmare, in case you haven't noticed.'

He still gripped the wheel as though he was choking the steering out of it. Mia wanted to laugh. He just looked so correct and desperate, with his pastel jumper folded round his neck like a French exchange student, even though it was the middle of the night.

'Have I said something funny?'

He asked her to look in the glove compartment for a packet of Nurofen and swallowed a couple dry. His small, involuntary bleat of panic as the capsules stuck in his throat almost set her off again. Neither of them spoke again until they were on the outskirts of Newquay.

'I suppose you could say it's history repeating itself,' said Nigel. 'First my mother . . .'

Mia stared. 'Did she work for Patrick? I didn't know . . .'

'Holly,' he said. 'I meant Holly. You know, Mum was a bit of a bolter.'

'What's that?'

'Running away.' His tone had dried up. 'Never mind.'

They were just coming off the second roundabout. As the car straightened, Mia saw a girl, picked out by a streetlight at the exit beyond the one they'd just taken.

'Holly!'

Holly reared round, then, seeing them brake, started to run off, heavily. She held the mobile—Louise's—in her hand. Swearing, Nigel reversed back up to the roundabout and manoeuvred to follow—there were no other cars to stop him. The filter road was dark and at first Mia thought they'd lost her again, that she'd pitched into a hedge and taken off across the fields. Bolted. Approaching a bend, twin lights arced towards them as a car swooped from the opposite direction and there Holly stood, solid in the middle of the road, blinking at the sudden flash-bright swathe of hedgerow as Mia screamed uselessly and the speeding car struck her, catapulting the handset from her fingers to shatter on the tarmac a moment before she bounced off the bonnet and rolled down next to it, broken.

June 5th 1982

Dear Tony,

Let there be no mistake, I was appalled by last night's perf. In the month since I ~~saw~~ last saw it, the play has changed out of recognition. The flags make the stage look like a fucking street party. Putting Wilson in a skirt and giving him a handbag and headscarf, although greeted with wild laughter by the audience, totally skews his speech. It can only be a matter of time before it's a full-blown Thatcher impression. Christopher ad libbed 'Goose Green' in the Act 1 litany and got the laugh of the night—that middle-class roar of self-congratulation that chills my blood. I don't care about box office, I don't care about the audience, I do care very much that my play has been hijacked as some sort of topical panto.

A hit's a hit, I hear you say. Obviously, the fact that all these embellishments have taken place without my consent speaks volumes. I would have

come in today, but Sara and I are
off to bloody Leeds. I'll be back by
tonight. Phone me once you get this.

Patrick

PS Carbon sent to the Board.

The first time Mia caught Louise on the landline, she assumed she was checking in with the hospital about Holly, but the face Louise pulled as Mia passed, acknowledgement mixed with embarrassment, implied a less businesslike transaction. When the calls continued, Mia's next thought was that she was ringing her son in Leeds. It was understandable, if a bit cheeky. Louise must have decided it was worth the money saved by not using her mobile, because there was no privacy in the hallway. The phone in Patrick's study shared the same line, but Louise was never going to venture in there, so she had to mutter her conversation where anyone moving through the lower part of the house—i.e., Mia—could hear. Even then, Mia's attention wasn't crucially drawn until one morning when she was coming downstairs and Louise turned into the receiver and lowered her speech so incriminatingly that Mia could only assume she was saying something about her. She strained to catch it.

'Those sort of vanilla wafers.'

Perhaps not, then. 'Not tea, no.' Another pause, then excitedly, 'Yes, yes that's right!'

Reaching the kitchen door, Mia glanced back up the corridor. Louise arched into the black handset, its ancient cord stretched tight, nodding at whatever was being said with transformative, eager engagement. She looked like she was being fed something.

It was possible that Louise had friends. She didn't have a boyfriend, Mia knew that, although her ex had turned up when she'd contacted him about Holly in the first few days after the accident. Warren, he was called. He was shaven-headed, mainly silent and about the same size as Louise; standing side by side, they had looked like a giant cruet set, him the salt and Louise the pepper. Louise's deferential tone during the calls didn't suggest a chat with him, or any other friend or lover. Who, then?

Over the next days Mia monitored Louise's phone activities with irresistible interest. She didn't say anything to Patrick; it wasn't worth the rage. Even immediately following the accident, he had been unsympathetic to Louise's need to use the house as a base close to the hospital where Holly was in intensive care. Louise remained mild, but she remained, coming back at odd hours for a bath and change of clothes, occasionally staying the night after Holly was out of danger, or catching up on sleep during the day, driving the forty-mile round trip to the hospital in Launceston in the ancient car Warren had brought down from Yorkshire for her. However foul Patrick was, swearing at her, kicking doors shut she had just opened, telling her continually that she was a cuckoo in the nest, she responded with depressed but persistent unamenability. At least now that Holly had started physical rehab and her recovery was cause for frail optimism, there was the possibility of transferring her care up north.

With all this deranged family stuff in full flow, Patrick wasn't quite as grateful to Mia as he had been. In fact, he could be intensely irritable and therefore irritating, riding her about everything from the colour of his toast to the accents of TV newsreaders. There was also the whole thing he'd started about her going out. Whenever she left the house, even just to wheel the rubbish out to the end of the drive on collection day, he always demanded to know where she was going. It wasn't as if Patrick's anxiety conferred even the implicit compliment of need for her company, since he still spent most of his day in his study. He just seemed to need the reassurance of her body around the place, like a dog. Or so she had thought, until the next time she had to ask him for unmentionables money.

'Distasteful . . .' Sliding notes across the kitchen table, Patrick's fingers stayed, trapping the cash. His expression was agelessly reasonable, as though discussing a third party. 'But you're old and educated enough to know the meaning of quid pro quo, my love.'

Well, not the Latin exactly, but it meant someone wanting to shag you, didn't it?

'I mean company, not molestation. A bit of human warmth.'

Apparently he wanted her to share his bed, 'no more'. Mia took the money and continued to sleep on the sofa in the den. She knew she would be able to fend him off. But the next day, she updated her CV and began to send off exploratory emails (language schools, a cooks' agency, one hopeful application for a magazine subeditor's job). While she waited for replies, she doggedly continued to put the house in order, entirely for her own satisfaction. The time had been passing, and she needed a plan. Particularly now it seemed that Patrick had had one all along.

One night, in sleepless panic about her future, Mia got up to make herself a herbal tea and was startled to discover Louise, crouched like a teenager with her back against the wall by the hall table, the elderly phone cradled down on her lap. As before, she appeared to be listening more than she was talking. As soon as she saw Mia, she lumbered to her feet, and in that moment, as Louise replaced the phone on the table and told her communicant that she would have to go, Mia's skin goose-pimpled. She hurried by, fully expecting Louise to follow her into the kitchen with an explanation, but in the time it took her to boil the kettle, shivering, Louise had disappeared back to bed.

Frustratingly, the hall phone was so old it lacked a redial function. Carrying her tea, Mia crept into the nicotine chill of Patrick's study, where the technology was marginally less antique. Safe within the searing little cone of light cast by Patrick's Anglepoise, she lifted the receiver. Around her, the house made its noises. She looked away from Sara's smile, its mystery held in the photo frame beside the lamp. Her teeth were chattering. Just who might answer if she revisited Louise's call? She replaced the receiver, conscious of an attempt to be as quiet as possible.

In the morning, bathed and rational, Mia marched into the study and punched redial. The number was for a premium-rate line to a psychic, although it took some pound-squandering minutes for her to manoeuvre through enough option buttons for this to become intelligible. She saw no reason not to raise the matter with Louise. Since Holly's accident, Louise had contributed nothing to the household, either financially or in terms of her labour. Mia didn't miss the sloppy pasta bakes, but she felt there was a principle being abused, and Louise's secrecy suggested she knew she was taking the piss. Really, Mia was protecting Patrick. He was an old man, after all.

She found Louise in the disused pantry that housed the washing machine, off the kitchen. Either too large or too inflexible to bend in the confined space, Louise sat on the floor, legs splayed ahead of her, posting clothes into the open drum like a scaled-up toddler with an educational toy.

'Did you want some washing doing?'

Mia didn't beat around the bush, as her own mother would say. She'd taken note of the premium-rate charges and recited them to Louise. Confronted with the evidence, Louise froze, holding a limp bundle of leggings in mid-air. Mia had noticed that she could only do one thing at a time.

'I'll reckon up with Patrick,' Louise said. 'It'll all be on the bill. Of course I will.'

'Well, that's okay, if it happens.' Mia found herself reluctant to forgo an argument.

'All the bills,' said Louise, 'the heating and that. I want to pay my way.' She kneaded the leggings, now in her lap.

'Those phone lines,' said Mia. 'You know they're just a rip-off.'

'Oh some of them are, of course,' Louise agreed.

'Why would you waste your money?'

'I've found someone really good,' Louise maintained. 'Really proper. Not like some of them. Kamila's definitely got the gift. She could even tell me stuff about Holly and that.'

'But Holly's alive.'

'A good psychic, they'll tell you all sorts. About the future. Stuff about you, even, she's told me.' Louise's gaze slid up from the leggings to Mia. 'She thinks you're alike, you see.'

'Sorry?'

'*Mum*. She's been communicating a lot about you. Nothing bad!'

From the floor, Louise stretched to pat Mia on the shin. Her eyes danced. Mia took an instinctive step back.

'She's given you her blessing. Because she was worried about Patrick being looked after, but now she knows he's got you, so she can be at peace, like. She says, "She's like me."'

So that's what it was. For a few months during her first year of university, Mia had worked for a sex chatline. A psychic's punter might demand more freewheeling invention than the sad wankers Mia had been instructed to string along, but she felt sure the underlying ethos was identical.

'These people will say anything to keep you talking. Trust me.'

'Well, we're all entitled to our beliefs.'

Louise resumed loading her washing, with the same unreachable aplomb she deployed when Patrick started shouting at her.

Sara speaking.

Instead of making soup for lunch, Mia picked up her bag and left the house without stopping to knock on Patrick's study door and let him know. He'd live. Getting out was pure relief, into the bracing November cold. As Mia walked up to the main road, she half-expected a toot behind her from Louise's rusty Nissan, making the daily trip to the hospital. Mia was prepared to reject the offer of a lift, but the car hadn't appeared by the time she turned on to the verge of the dual carriageway. She headed off in the opposite direction.

There was an attenuated bus service to Newquay, but Mia walked the full seven miles, flayed increasingly by the wind. It was crazy, living somewhere so remote without a car. Patrick had never learned to drive, of course, and although, according to Nigel, Sara had always acted as chauffeur, she had stopped driving for the last years of her life, despite the viable-looking Peugeot still standing in the garage. Mia, having given it a cursory inspection, thought its trade-in value was probably nil.

With her circulation speeding and a massive appetite, Mia felt herself again. The walk had taken over two hours, making Holly's feat on the night of her accident even more remarkable. Passing the second roundabout, Mia stared determinedly ahead, refusing to notice the patch of road where, during their terrible wait for help, Nigel had got down and cradled Holly's still head, using his folded jumper as a cushion. Mia had kept talking to her, shocked words of meaningless consolation, unable to touch or look as she looped up to the junction and back on the pretext of checking for the ambulance. The one horror-film glimpse of Holly's illogically splayed legs, the gloss of blood across her white face, had been unbearable. The paramedics had assumed that Mia would want to go with Holly in the ambulance, called her 'your sister', although Mia had quickly put them right. Given that unwelcome flashback to the moment of damage, it was incredible the doctors had been able to pin Holly back together so confidently. She was healing. No doubt Louise thought that this process had been abetted by Sara, who was apparently watching over them all.

She thinks you're alike, you see.

Mia marched into the first Costa she saw. Waiting for her molten panini to cool, she brushed aside inherited muffin crumbs to make a suitable space on the table and took out her leather-bound notebook. Also a good pen. A rollerball, which she preferred to a ballpoint. The trick with lists was to start with a couple of things already accomplished. *Course*, Mia wrote, then immediately ticked it off. Strictly speaking, although her dealings with Newcastle were squared away, there was the matter of her graduate loan, but she was hardly about to sully the immediate simplicity of her list. *Mum*, she proceeded. This also warranted an immediate tick, since she had sent her mother a card on her recent birthday, making an unspecified promise to visit.

Kitchen came next. With an increasing sense of redundancy, Mia inked a dash and added a question mark. She knew that manoeuvring Patrick into agreeing to any kind of work, let alone the renovation she had extensively envisaged, would take serious and unavailing effort. He had even put a stop to her very basic decorating plans once he knew how much it would cost. It wasn't just that Patrick couldn't care less. She knew now that she had been bamboozled by the good furniture and the house around it, while failing to read the more accurate message of their neglect. She had simply assumed that Patrick was mean and his late wife chaotic, and that she'd be able to cajole him into spending in the same way that she'd finally got him to eat garlic. But his scrimping, own-brand ways weren't just habits. He was, it turned out, as broke as she was.

Well, this wasn't entirely true. Through the forensic ransacking of the paperwork she had cleared from every surface, Mia was stunned to discover that Patrick and Sara had never mitigated their hardships with even a normal level of debt.

'Not even a credit card?'

'Fetters of capitalism. Cut 'em up as soon as they sent 'em.'

It was beyond own-brand, or not taking holidays. Accordingly,

Mia had applied for a couple of credit cards in Patrick's name and was working up to getting him to sign them, for his own good.

Pen hovering over her list, she forbore to write Patrick's name, even as a sub-category of *kitchen*, although she did finally scribble *finance??*, from which was born *bank*. To accomplish anything there would have to be a chunky loan. Given that all she needed was the first sniff of a job offer to send her on her way, even research at the level of price-comparison websites was pointless. Mia scored the entire entry through.

Mia nibbled her panini. *Job*, she wrote finally. No dash, no question mark, and definitely, despite all those emails, no tick. Looking up, she saw that the Costa employee who had served her, a post-adolescent boy with dark circles under his darker eyes and a misguided directional haircut that angled to conceal one ear and was shaved above the other, was lingering under the pretext of clearing the next table to watch her write. It was the post-lunch lull.

'Busy.'

The word was bottom-heavy with an accent, possibly Polish. Mia flashed him a dismissive smile.

'You need?' He offered her the napkin dispenser he was lifting to wipe beneath. Politely, she hoisted the thin napkin on her panini plate. 'No thank you.'

He mimicked writing. 'Studying?'

Capping her pen, Mia shook her head, whisked the list into her bag and reached for her scarf. The boy hovered, possibly on the verge of telling her that he was a student himself, or wanted to be: psychology, perhaps, or business studies. Although if it was business, why was he working in a Costa?

With a smile full of aggravating irony, the boy tried to fix her gaze. 'Something more interesting than studying, maybe.'

She had a vision of her own future, learning to flourish frothed milk into the calligraphic leaf on top of a flat white. *Chocolate on that?*

Mia shouldered her bag. 'Everything about me is more interesting than you can possibly fucking imagine.'

She didn't look back as she made for the door. She was so much better than all of it. She always had been.

After an undermotivated tour of the less tacky shops, the acquisition of some interiors magazines that would have earned her another tick on the kitchen portion of her list if she hadn't scrubbed it out, and a maintenance trip to Tesco, Mia took a cab back to the house. It was still quite early, and she was relieved not to see Louise's car parked outside. As she paid the cab driver, Patrick appeared from the back of the house. He was shouting.

'Everything all right with the old boy?' asked the driver, a middle-aged man who had spent the journey telling her about his cholesterol levels.

'I think he was just wondering where I'd gone.' Mia terminated their transaction with a couple of pound coins and straightened up from the car door to withstand Patrick. It would be the usual thing. Sure enough, he started before the minicab had even negotiated the turn in the drive.

'Where the fuck have you been?'

She told him, briskly headed towards the back door, in no mood. Patrick hurried to keep astride with her, the slight swing of the Tesco bags batting him away as she manoeuvred them through the doorway. Backing round to accomplish this brought his face into proper view. Mia's first thought was that his eyes were watering from the wind, then she realised that he was weeping.

'Patrick.'

She had looked into his study, she lied, but he had been asleep.

She should have left him a note. Or perhaps, to prevent this happening again, he might finally learn how to dial her mobile, which had been switched on all afternoon?

'I don't want to learn how to use your bloody mobile, just don't do it again, you stupid little bitch!'

The margins of Mia's tenderness contracted. Silently, she triaged groceries from their bags on to the table, before putting them away in cupboards and fridge, showing him her back.

'I will not live like this!' Patrick roared.

Continuing to ignore him, Mia stacked cans of tuna, taking the time to align them exactly. Behind her, she sensed movement as Patrick took a peevish swipe at a box of eggs. She wheeled into a stretch that caught them as they left the tabletop, surprising herself with her agility. Patrick scrabbled to pull the box from her, his massive hands crushing the cardboard as they tussled, her gasping and him grunting with animal effort until, at the sound of cracking shells Mia gave way, leaving Patrick to hoist the egg box one-handed above his head in a pose that was equal parts childish triumph and melodramatic threat. As he held this ridiculous position, a clear, spunky gout of egg white gathered from the lowest corner of the box and glopped down on to the shoulder of his jumper.

Mia laughed. Not as a weapon, but in rare true amusement, as happened to her sometimes, the way it had with Nigel when he gulped Nurofen on the night of Holly's accident. Patrick touched his shoulder, exclaimed, '*Shit!*' and momentarily panicked her by also bursting into laughter. Laughing, seeing him laugh, Mia felt something like joy. No future, no past, just this.

'Oh Christ.' Patrick steadied himself against the table for a few breaths, knuckles down on the scarred wood. 'Forgive me, darling girl. Jesus.'

And he gathered her into his stinking old jumper, but she liked the smell, of whisky and fags and him, and even though the wool was full of holes it was actually cashmere. She avoided the egg white. He moved her back, looking for something in her face. Finding it, he kissed her, properly.

That night, having troubled to change the sheets, she followed him up to bed.

June 11th 1982

Dear Tony,

Good to see you and Penny yesterday, and thanks for the lunch. I hope your hangover isn't as wretched as mine. Your theory about the better vintages doesn't seem to obtain, but there was a glory in the experiment.

Forgive the arse-aching. It's not just stubbornness. I may not subscribe to the idea of an immortal soul, but I do have an artistic conscience. Indeed, it's the only conscience I do have. A small thing, but mine own . . .

To reiterate: Bloody Empire isn't, never has been, and never will be a play about the Falklands. Although I can accept an element of serendipity in the timing of the production, I am very much inclined to look the gift horse, as you put it, in the mouth. A transfer to the West End may be lucrative, but really what could it profit beyond our bank accounts? Dancing cats are one thing, gilding our reputations with the blood of the fallen, another.

And yet, and yet. There can be no doubt but, like everything in this fallen world, conscience has its price.

God help me, I may have discovered
exactly what it is. Man the telephone,
Mephistopheles.

Yours aye,
Patrick

PS. Apologies from Sara. She's been
rather tired lately.

Then

1983

SINCE OXFORD in summer term—Trinity term—was so obviously close to heaven, with the green college gardens, and drinks parties, and Shakespeare productions and drinks parties in college gardens, and punting, and Pimm's, and rowing tournaments, and balls, and long, starlit nights out on the window ledges of rooms or in obscure meadows at parties, so many parties, Nigel's exclusion from all these forms of paradise was particularly tormenting. It was like one endless production of *A Midsummer Night's Dream* (which he had recently seen at Wadham, staged in the gloaming at the edge of the lake), in which he, an anti-Titania, had been forcibly unenchanted and left alone to see flaccid strings of mint in the warm, weak Pimm's, wheeze asthmatically in the gardens however much he deployed his inhaler, and everywhere hear the confident, opinionated braying of his snogging, rutting cohort, their wholehearted hedonism failing to conceal from him its underpinning of untransformed self-advancement.

In the first month there had at least been exams—Mods—running alongside all of this, but now they were over and enjoyment was unconfined. Nigel slightly regretted the lack of an excuse to stay in the library even a little of the time, but the library, so crammed with territorial, hollow-eyed finalists for most of the year, was now deserted, the liberated finalists having preceded the first-years in abandonment to all this noisy pleasure. Despite spending his mornings asleep (in common with most members of the college), the days were sadistically long. Work had distracted him from his failure to extract any value from Oxford apart from the pale appreciation of his law tutors for his uninspired reliability in producing his weekly essays. This apart, he may as well have been studying law anywhere else in the country, redbricked or concreted, although when he was feeling particularly desperate he reminded himself that value would be added once he came to the stage of applying to law firms, so long as he did himself justice in exams. He also reminded himself of how very proud he assumed he had made his mother, Auntie B and Louise.

He was, though, feeling particularly desperate, which was why he had accepted Toby's sister's invitation to the picnic at St Hilda's. Entering the porter's lodge after a doctor's appointment—he had been wondering if he had a virus and the brisk GP had told him that he was probably drinking too much and not eating properly—Nigel had almost missed the note in his pigeonhole, mixed in with photocopied fliers for garden plays and Undercroft bops, a scrawl on a torn half-sheet of pale green notepaper. The hurried writing, its comely, feminine flow, was enough to provoke fantasies of ending the evening in Toby's sister's narrow St Hilda's bed. Her name was Zoë, and she was in her second year. They had met just once, when Toby had visited Oxford the previous term (Hilary), on a break from the London crammer where his parents had sent him after he had tanked his A-levels at St Christopher's. Toby had brought her along with him when he had arranged to meet Nigel for a drink at the Eagle and Child.

Zoë was almost as tall as her brother, with the same hectic complexion but apparently none of his good nature. In common with all the girls he had met at Oxford, her wrists and knuckles were occluded by her overstretched jumper sleeves, the excess of which she kept gathered into each palm, as if she was either perpetually cold or—less likely—shy. She had barely stayed to finish her half (which Nigel had paid for), annoyed about some unfathomable but clearly boyfriend-related arrangement that she accused Toby of fouling up by arriving late, and had left abruptly after making a call from the pub's payphone, borrowing the change to do so from Nigel, along with a further two pounds for the cigarette machine. So it was surprising to be invited to bring a bottle, 'pref sparkling', to her picnic. There was a hand-drawn map at the bottom of the sheet, guiding him to a riverside spot behind the St Hilda's grounds.

'Any difficulties with girls?' the GP had asked him, while grudgingly filling out the forms for a blood test. Nigel had said no. The briskness of her tone, her middle age and utilitarian haircut, didn't invite any kind of confidence, although there was an even more alarming glimmer of sympathy behind her manner.

Nigel took an antihistamine, bought an unchilled bottle of Asti Spumante and, as the sky's colour leached into night, headed up towards Iffley Road. Hilda's was all-girls, so his chances were good, even if Zoë herself had a boyfriend. He reminded himself not to get too drunk. He really felt like getting drunk.

By the riverbank, there were far more guests than he had been expecting. Although a few token picnic blankets scattered around the field bore trampled quiches, open packets of crisps and plundered punnets of strawberries, Nigel was undeceived. He recognised the same, rolling party he had been fruitlessly attending for the last three weeks. A boombox parked by the strawberries played *Off the Wall*, and he immediately spotted four members of his own college: two historians, a physicist and a prat wearing a trilby and earring whose subject he assumed to be English, trying to chat up the Hilda's girls. Still, the ratio remained promising. Reassuring himself that the bulge of his inhaler was intact in his front right trouser pocket, he went to look for Zoë.

She was pissed and, therefore, cheerful. Oddly, her upbeat mood actually decreased her resemblance to her brother. This may have been because she was wearing eye make-up and looked disarmingly pretty when she smiled. Nigel realised that she was probably a full two years older than him, since he was one of the few people he had met who hadn't taken what he had learned to call a gap year.

'I'm doing it,' Zoë announced, hooking her slender ankles and dropping to the grass cross-legged. 'I said it was a picnic and as far as I'm concerned it means not having to stand up all fucking night.'

Nigel was relieved to sit down. For one thing, it made the disparity in their heights less marked. He refused the packet of Silk Cut Zoë waved at him, and busied himself in untwisting the wire on the cork of the Asti Spumante. Something he had learned since he'd been at Oxford—possibly the only useful thing so far that wasn't Tort—was the gentle touch needed in releasing corks of this kind, the steadying thumb.

'There are more glasses somewhere. Plastic.' Zoë waved out at the grass. It was beginning to get properly dark; points of cigarettes and the odd spliff glow-wormed the view, flaring with each inhalation. Zoë added hers as she reached to get a light from the friend she had been talking to when Nigel approached, a shorter girl with lots of tumbling dark hair. Nigel decided not to bother finding a glass. He took a slug of the warmly fizzy wine and passed it to Zoë. She added some to the plastic cup nested in the dip of her curled legs and handed it along to her friend, who fielded her mass of hair back behind one shoulder before she took the bottle. This gesture placed her, for Nigel, as the editor of a student newspaper; he had loitered at the back of just one editorial meeting at the beginning of the first—Michaelmas—term, listening to her self-assured spiel, but lacked any answering confidence to pitch a story at the end of the same meeting. He thought her name might be Imogen. Or Cressida. Something obscurely Shakespearean, definitely. Beyond her was another girl, fine-featured, frosty. Smiling into the darkness, Nigel felt the familiar sinking totality of their lack of interest in him as he indicated that this girl, too, should have a swig of wine. It would be worse when he spoke. Although he had submerged his accent as much as possible in his years at St Christopher's, there was always someone to ask if he was northern, who had a cousin at Ampleforth they expected him to know.

'So, Cally,' said Zoë, 'Nigel's stepdad is Patrick Conway. You know. *Bloody Empire*. Isn't your aunt in it or something?'

At this Imogen/Cressida rearranged her hair in order to get a better look at him. Cally, with the fine face, stubbed the last of her cigarette on the grass and smiled, revealing snaggled white teeth.

'Really? God, it's extreme, isn't it? I saw it when it was at the National and I didn't have a clue what was going on. I can't believe she goes on every night, like . . . months of it. And now they're in the West End and everything, talking about taking it to America . . .'

She rubbed at her face, looking up at him impishly. He had been wrong about her; she was all friendliness. Her smile was lovely. And he'd seen her aunt's tits.

'I don't really get it, to be honest.'

'Me neither,' he said, smiling back.

'So what's it like,' asked Cressida/Imogen, with warm, competitive attention, as she curated her hair, 'having Patrick Conway as your dad?'

All three of them were looking at him now, waiting for him to speak. He didn't bother to correct them about the stepfather confusion.

'Extreme.'

He decided it would be okay to get incredibly drunk.

FOR LOUISE, FIFTEEN was turning out to be worse than fourteen or even thirteen, a daily battle of wrongness. In her bedroom, she lived close to her reflection, tallying her many flaws and eruptions. She hoisted the Boots magnifying mirror at extreme angles, desperate to catch an unfamiliar, partial glimpse of herself that might transmute into acceptability. Sometimes, with a slide of the eye, it worked. Mostly though, she despaired. She had nothing that gave you power as a fifteen-year-old girl: skin, hair, tits, legs, clothes, confidence, sarcasm, brains, malice, promiscuity, friends, money, parents with money, parents. She hated Auntie B, and hated herself more for hating her, but couldn't stop it, or stop showing how much she hated her. School was a filler in the week, fending off the greater boredom of the weekend. The time she didn't spend at school she mainly spent in her bedroom, communing with the mirror, masturbating to baroque fantasies with a royalist tinge (the aftermath of the Charles and Diana wedding was still intense in their household), or eating multiple, sickening bars of chocolate. When it got too cold in her room or she became too disgusted with herself, Louise went downstairs and watched telly with Auntie B. Unless the programme was unusually absorbing, she compensated for her parting from the mirror by brailling her fingers along her latest crop of spots, making them, as Auntie B never failed to tell her, worse.

It was in all ways a dreadful life. To escape it, Louise had become interested in the possibilities of her soul, which she assumed to be the invisible part of her dedicated to hectoring the shortcomings of her body and its behaviours. The notion of the soul was chalked up on the board in RE as unassailably as a Pythagorean equation by Mr Redstone, whose long weasel body, everyone knew, was up to no good with a sixth-former, despite him being married. It wasn't anything purveyed by Mr Redstone that appealed to Louise. Her interest in what she had no idea could be called a spiritual life had been piqued by an interview she'd read in Auntie B's *Daily Express*, where an American rock star had mentioned his devotion to Transcendental Meditation. He'd made it sound like magic. Better yet, he'd made it sound like magic that more or less allowed you to fly away from your body. Louise had followed this bewitching possibility to the library, which yielded only a slim, worthily brown cloth-covered book from the 1950s, part of a series that included vegetarianism and Buddhism as subjects. The book's arid lack of glamour was disappointing, as was its failure to mention transcendence, but she put it on her ticket anyway.

The mirror, masturbation and chocolate eating were now interspersed with Louise's attempts to empty her mind and feel herself at the bottom of the sea, as the book instructed, directing bubbles up to the surface, each of them containing a cluttering thought newly released from her mind. There seemed to be an endless proliferation of bubbles, some of them quite difficult to budge from the ocean floor, and more than once Louise had fallen asleep in the attempt. She knew she wouldn't persevere. She hoped, though, that the effort might make her more interesting, that when Mum and Patrick paid their next visit, she could drop her new hobby into the conversation and Patrick would see her in a different, compatible light. She wouldn't call it a hobby, of course: hobbies were the kind of thing Patrick despised. Little England, he'd probably call them, as he did most things enjoyed by other people. Holidays, parties and TV were all Little England. Also, caravans, pets, gardens, paying to see gardens, and many kinds of food, particularly food doled out in pots or saucers into individual portions. The word 'portions', in fact, was itself very Little England, according to Patrick. A portion in a ramekin, served by anyone prepared to use the word 'ramekin', would probably make his head blow off.

'I've started meditating.'

The first time Louise broached it, she was in the back of the car. Mum was having trouble with the one-way system that led out of town and Patrick was barking at her because she was driving up a narrow street towards an oncoming Volkswagen.

'For fuck's sake!'

Patrick had never learned to drive, and was a nervous passenger. Mum was a bad driver, but calm. She started a multifaceted turn, grinding the gears. Louise sat back in her seat, feeling foolish. When she mentioned the subject again, at the restaurant, she pretended it was the first time she'd said it.

'I've started meditating.'

They were having a drink before lunch, in the bar. Auntie B's presence had been dispensed with a few years previously, when she had made a sour comment about not being needed as the life and soul, and Patrick had amazed her by agreeing that the three of them could do without her. Mum had managed to stop it turning into a proper row, but since then Auntie B had seen them off, saying she knew when she wasn't wanted. Now, Patrick and Mum were both drinking sherry out of shapely little glasses the fake parchment menu called schooners, and Louise sipped warmish pineapple juice. There were ships' steering wheels and polished brass bells and dark wood. They had never been to this particular restaurant before. It was, Patrick had remarked when they arrived, almost nice.

She tried it again; third time lucky. 'I've started meditating.'

'Well.'

Mum unloosed her bright scarf, eager yet uninterested. Patrick paused in settling his iffy disc into the spindle-backed chair.

'*Meditating?*'

'I got a book from the library. You have to . . . to empty your mind. It's quite hard, actually, 'cos even when you're not thinking, you kind of catch yourself thinking about not thinking, so that's another thought, and you have to get rid of it, and if you're thinking of *that*—'

'Why on earth would you want to empty your mind?'

Patrick didn't mean anybody, he meant her. He meant her mind was already empty enough. Louise touched the tender place on her jaw where a spot was ripening under the skin.

'To, to free it of worldly concerns.'

He enjoyed this. Mum smiled back at him.

'And what Gurdjieffian voodoo has captured your imagination, Louise?'

She had no idea what this meant, but the silkiness of Patrick's tone was recognisably dangerous.

'The Beatles did it,' she proffered.

'There you go.' This was to Mum. 'The *Beatles* did it.'

'Actually,' Mum said, bracing her forearms against her place-mat. 'We've got news of our own.'

She'd forgotten that she'd already told Auntie B in a letter about her and Patrick moving out of London and buying a house in Cornwall with the money from Patrick's play going into the West End. Louise pretended it was all a surprise as Mum talked about the house, and how big it was, and how they'd be able, finally, to have her and Nidge to stay and have a proper family Christmas. Mum flushed pink talking about how beautiful it was, by the sea, and Louise began to feel quite excited herself, while Patrick and Mum, but mainly Patrick, finished their bottle of red ('passable little plonk'). When she ran out of Cornwall, Mum continued to carry the burden of the conversation with a familiar set of consequenceless questions. Louise loved any evidence of curiosity about herself, however formulaic, so she didn't mind the stop-start, and she was enjoying her food.

When the waitress brought the second bottle, Mum raised her glass, still filled from the first. Louise couldn't remember ever seeing her smile so much.

'To Nidge,' she said, as was traditional, 'and to a family Christmas.' Which wasn't. Particularly as there was months to go until then. Patrick didn't join in the toast, which was his own tradition.

'Meditation . . . the flight of the mind.'

He was chewing the last of his steak. Louise and Mum had moved on to talking about winter coats. Both of them tensed at his tone.

'It's exactly as I've always said, the sixties were a sort of collective cultural adolescence . . .' Vehemently, he rattled his knife and fork on to the plate and pushed himself back from the table. 'You have the excuse of actual adolescence, I suppose, but you may as well know you're about twenty years too late in terms of the culture, dear.'

'Oh Pat, leave her alone.'

'*Meditation*. Mental masturbation. You'll go blind. *Spiritually* speaking, of course. Stick to the other is my advice.'

Louise was horrified to see people looking round. No one talked like Patrick up here, either in accent, volume, or subject matter. Pinking, she concentrated on the ridges on a chip left on her plate. Of course it was impossible for anyone to suspect what she got up to with Viscount Linley. Patrick couldn't read her mind.

'It's important though, Christ. If not our minds, what the fuck do we have? Why, of all things, at this point in human history, would we be seeking to abnegate our individuality? Tell me'—she could feel him glaring at her—'what is there, Louise—no, I'm really interested—what is there but the *world*?'

'Well, we were all young once. And you forget how the world can seem sometimes. You don't want a pudding, do you?' Mum turned to her.

Louise did want a pudding, very much. She'd been thinking about it all morning.

'No thanks.'

They brought chocolate mints with the coffee, Elizabeth Shaws. Her mother didn't eat any and Patrick only had one, so Louise nibbled through the toothpaste-flavoured gravelliness of three remaining in the saucer. She refrained from the last mint only in case Patrick commented, which he was clearly in the mood to do. He was sipping an Irish coffee in another ladylike glass, larger this time. The stripe of cream at the top of the drink whitened his full upper lip as he drank; he was beyond noticing.

'Such a relief to be out of that pokey little flat,' said Mum. 'You won't believe it when you see the rooms. Rooms and rooms, aren't there, Pat? You'll have to choose one for yourself, Lou.'

'Bollocks.' It had reached that stage. Although it often reached that stage on their outings, usually it was to do with Patrick's work, or the government, not with anything directly related to or aimed at Louise. Today though, she had set him off, just by trying to make conversation. What was so wrong with meditation? She wasn't hurting anyone.

'Bollocks!' Louder on the repeat, it was an invitation, or an incitement. Either way, Louise felt, staring at the dimpled foil of the single disc left on the saucer, that it was intolerable. Practically everyone in the restaurant was staring now.

'I'm entitled to my beliefs,' she said primly. It was something she'd seen on TV, or heard; she thought it would work better than saying she wasn't hurting anyone.

'You are not fucking *entitled*, you stupid little bitch!'

She may as well have doused Patrick in petrol and put a match to him.

'Patrick—'

'*Entitled*, Christ! Where did that come from, a fucking Christmas cracker? Jesus. You're entitled to have a brain in your little head, that's the only entitlement you have, love, and that's an obligation as well—and don't tell me what you believe because you and the lumpen majority don't have beliefs, you have fucking badges, little badges you sport instead of troubling yourself with any act of moral imagination—"Ban the Bomb"—that'll do, pin that one on, job done!'

A tough-faced waitress stopped to pick up the napkin that Patrick had dropped on the carpet and place it back on his plate. He didn't recognise the warning.

'Those aren't beliefs, love, they're fucking *mottos*. "Burn your bra"—ooh, how clever! You know, a bit of alliteration doesn't make something the sodding truth—'

Her mother put her hand on his. 'Enough.'

It was more than she usually had to do. Mum gave the waitress a settling look—*I'll deal with it*.

'If you don't start using this'—Patrick jabbed a finger over the table at her head; Louise flinched back—'you'll never be anything but a third-rate provincial little slapper, if you ever manage to find some gormless bastard desperate enough to give you a seeing to in the first place—'

Mum was standing, wrangling her coat across her shoulders, bending to pull her purse from her handbag. She nodded at the waitress. 'We'd like to pay.' She started to pull out five-pound notes that looked fresh from the bank. Her purse was swollen with them, the clasp strained.

Louise also stood. Suddenly, Patrick was alone. He stirred himself to catch up with them. As soon as he flailed an arm behind him, Mum was there to help him eel it into his raincoat, the maroon one he'd always worn. She didn't want him to strain his bad back. Louise saw Patrick look at Mum, but her concentration on his coat gave nothing away. She smoothed it over his shoulders, dusting away a little dandruff. He faltered.

'None of my business anyway,' he concluded. 'Thank God. No spawn of mine . . . You do what you like—good luck to you!'

With a terminating shovel of his arms, this sign-off finally acknowledged the audience gawping from the tables around them and put the blame on Louise. They manoeuvred to look.

'Need a slash.'

As Patrick stalked out, Louise fingered her jaw. She was memorising the carpet, the interlocking edges of its baronial crests in soiled autumn shades. Gradually, she felt the attention of the room leave her. She dared a glance at Mum, who, intent on a nonexistent horizon, was vaguely teasing her fingers through the ends of her hair.

'Why do you put up with him?'

It was worse than anything she'd said about meditation, but perhaps she hadn't said it out loud. Mum gazed, unhearing. Louise didn't repeat herself.

In the car, Mum and Patrick discussed the building work that had started on the outskirts of Chapeltown. Patrick thought it was pointless, because all the Common Market incentives in the world wouldn't attract thinking human beings to a shithole like this. Mum directed a few comments into the back, about how much Louise would love Cornwall. Louise allowed herself to drift away, down at the bottom with her mental bubbles. She just wanted it to be over, and soon enough it was. Mum and Patrick had had their cup of tea with Auntie B when they arrived to pick her up, so she ran by herself from the idling car into the house. Mum, already shifting into gear, bipped the horn in a final salute as Louise opened the front door with her Yale key. She was shouting something that Louise didn't catch properly at first.

'Christmas!'

Back in her bedroom, Louise squeezed the unready spot until it bled. She didn't care about bloody Christmas. Weighing Mum's refusal to meet Patrick's eye as she dealt with his coat, she knew Mum had been as angry as Patrick, but whether it was at Patrick for his outburst or Louise for provoking it, she couldn't tell. She shifted the weight of this apprehension, trying to clear the ocean floor, back up to the surface where it could pop and disappear, but it kept getting stuck, somewhere near her stomach. Maybe it had been her fault. Mum and Patrick, Patrick and Mum. Cornwall. Nigel. Eventually, inevitably, she fell asleep.

Part Three

Now

SPRING AGAIN

Mia's call was put through to Nigel at work. There had been a merciful hiatus in communication from what he and Sophie had taken to calling 'Down There', so his assistant was still, at his irritable request, establishing exactly who Mia was when Nigel himself realised and jumped on to the line, dismissing Diane and saying it was fine, he'd take the call.

He put aside the M & S duck wrap he was halfway through eating, while noting Mia's consideration in ringing him at lunchtime.

'Mia, what can I do for you?'

Nigel maintained a briskly professional tone. She was just about young enough to be his daughter, had his sexual history been altogether different.

'Are you around tomorrow? I'm coming to London. There's something I need to talk to you about.'

Nigel failed in his attempt to find this unexciting. He suggested lunch at a café near, but not incriminatingly close to, his office, as though he was doing something to be ashamed of. He hoped she would be wearing the boots.

He believed the expression to be that the gods laugh when men make plans, because he certainly wasn't the one laughing when, well into the first-coffee-and-emails stage of the next morning,

Nigel got the call from Sophie, full of ambient noise and panic, to say that she'd totally forgotten, hadn't she, Albie's bloody nursery was *shut* because of a bloody training day, and it bloody would be—yes sweetheart, just talking to Daddy—wouldn't it be the day she'd got theatre tickets for her and her mother, didn't he remember, she'd said at breakfast—Mum's birthday present, the matinee, they'd had a whole conversation about her and Nigel travelling back together (of course he remembered *now*, poor *her)*—so she was sorry, honey, she couldn't see any way round it because she'd rung round absolutely everyone, Jill was down with a stomach thing and she couldn't get hold of Tig—she'd just have to bring Albie into town with her and drop him at Nigel's office for a couple of hours, surely that was all right, wasn't it, couldn't the girls look after him if Nigel had to see clients? He was so sweet, they'd probably enjoy it, it would only be for a couple of hours, it was the thing at the Donmar, there wasn't even an interval, she'd checked.

So it was that Sophie arrived at the office just as Diane was doing the sandwich round Nigel had opted out of, hectic with makeup and jollying along a sceptical Albie and his accompanying Albie-sized bag of possible amusements. Diane and the office girls swooped. Nigel noted the reticence of Tamara Browning, their most recent graduate recruit, who had not only reassured him and the other partners interviewing her of her single status, but declared an unsolicited dislike of children. The firmness with which she closed her blond-wood office door against the cooings of welcome suggested this hadn't been said for effect, which augured well for the firm's investment.

Nigel had tried to warn Mia about the change of plan, but her phone seemed to have been switched off.

'I was in a quiet coach.'

She unwound lengths of scarf from her slender neck as he settled Albie next to him, facing Mia in the booth seats they'd managed to claim. Nigel pinioned Albie into the wall side so that he couldn't toddle out and create mayhem in the heaving, cramped space. Nigel had chosen the café at the recommendation of one of the younger partners, keen to avoid the more formal restaurants where he lunched clients and was likely to run into someone he knew. Looking around at the effortfully utilitarian décor, he wondered if he had got the right establishment. The clientele seemed very young, with odd bits of their hair shaved off and extensive beards on the men, and they were all dressed like extras from a period drama set in the American Depression. There was only one other man apart from himself in what he considered normal clothes.

The waitress recited the menu, which was unavailable in print, and involved lots of barbecued meat. Dirty food, the partner had called it—in itself an enticement. Sophie had fed Albie his lunch on the train, so he was interested in the chips Nigel ordered for him mainly as a medium for self-expression. Messy play, they called it at nursery. Mia showed about as much interest in the little boy as Tamara Browning had, which Nigel didn't hold against her. He made a half-joke about her liking children but not being able to manage a whole one.

'Excuse me?'

Mia's face was dead of amusement; she simply hadn't understood. Nigel shrugged a 'never mind' and tried to corral Albie's gargantuan chips into their side of the table surface. The waitress brought the adults their pulled-pork sandwiches, her miniature biceps bulging against the weight of the mounded platters. He had done the ordering, at Mia's suggestion; he saw her flinch as her portion was placed in front of her.

'So, Mia, what can uncle Nigel do for you?'

Mia considered her meat, glistening with rendered fat.

'Don't tell me—it's Louise.' He hadn't heard anything from

Louise in weeks, since she had told him Holly would soon be discharged from hospital. About bloody time. The girl had even spent Christmas in there, with Louise trekking up to share the festivities; what a day that must have been. He wondered if Mia had spent the holiday with her family.

'No, actually, it isn't Louise.' Mia took a sip of sparkling water. He'd ordered a Diet Coke, which he was keeping well clear of Albie's busy elbows.

'Then it must be Patrick.'

'In a way.' Mia smoothed her hair. Nigel noticed her nails: very short and clean, subtly manicured.

'He's asked me to marry him.'

The pork dried in his mouth. Of course, it was what he had been expecting. Why did it matter?

'I see.'

And then, in the afterwash of his disappointment, came a different swell. The house. Mia's eyes flicked away, as though in prescient distaste.

'I thought it was a good idea to talk to you about it, in case it's a problem.'

'Are you asking my permission?'

Mia put down her fork. Resmoothed her hair.

'I know there's still stuff to sort out about—your mum, and her will. And obviously it's all a bit soon.'

'Drawin'?' asked Albie.

'In a minute,' Nigel promised.

Mia looked at him properly. 'I mean, I'd wait, but Patrick says he's not getting any younger.'

This punched a laugh out of him. 'A whirlwind romance.'

'Is it a problem?'

Albie was pulling at his cuff. Nigel winkled down into the

backpack jammed by his legs for the notebook and pens Sophie had provided.

'I don't understand what you're asking me, Mia. You'll have to be more direct.'

Clearing a chip-free space, he settled Albie to work. Mia forked apart sticky strands of meat without lifting any to her mouth.

'I'm not sure exactly what's supposed to be happening with the house . . . and if Patrick getting married again—if that affects anything.'

Nigel savoured a heady moment of withheld knowledge. Why should he tell her? Now that the legalities had all been disentangled, with no small thanks to him, Patrick would be getting a letter. Let her find out everything she needed to know from her husband-to-be. By agreeing to marry the old bastard, Mia had forfeited the right to any favours from him.

The forceful scribble of Albie's pen squealed intolerably against the paper. Nigel caught hold of his arm. 'Not so hard, darling.' And then, to Mia, blandly, 'Has Patrick spoken to his solicitor lately? I would imagine he has all the hard facts.'

Mia's mouth tucked. She wasn't expecting to be thwarted.

'Do you think I'm mad, marrying Patrick?'

It wasn't a question he'd expected. Looking up, he saw something he'd never encountered in Mia's face before: vulnerability. She was so young. So perfectly fucking young.

'That's none of my business.'

'I mean—' She stopped, put down her fork. 'I'm not replacing your mother. I know how he felt about her.'

Nigel took a mouthful of coleslaw. It was vegetables, of a kind.

'I presume you haven't mentioned it to Louise. Getting married.'

Mia nudged her plate, apparently embarrassed. Her mouth made a smile. 'No, not yet.'

'Very wise. I'd let her get Holly home, if I were you.'

Mia nodded. His prospective mother-in-law. The gods must be wetting themselves by now. Nigel pushed away his own plate. He could feel the grease sitting at the top of his gut.

'Well,' he said, 'I wish you every happiness.'

Paddy–

You need to put the dish in the oven at least 25 minutes to heat through, gas 3. No longer than 40 or it will burn, don't forget. Carrots on stove you just boil five minutes there's salt already in the pan. Worcester sauce on table, yogurt in the fridge for afters. I'll be back to make supper.

S x

Ps. They didn't have the razors you asked for, but these are Wilkinsons too. If no good I will change at Boots.

LOUISE HAD ENDURED the different shape of every day since Holly had been hit by that car, the way a good morning could turn into a bad afternoon, an infinite night you were terrified to get to the end of in case she wasn't still with you by morning. With the signposts of washings and feedings and sleepings removed and replaced by the unpredictable incursion of tests and consultations, time lengthened, never your own, however much of it you were required to fill between the arbitrary, anxious periods of attention from layers of doctors. Even though faces and shift patterns became familiar, the passage of the long hours remained unique to each day. But in the past week, with the physios dropping in to see Holly, and Jamie finally coming down to visit, the days had suddenly turned back into days, grey and uniform. Driving out of the hospital car park, it was a surprise to see the blossom heavy on the trees. Weeks and weeks of now had suddenly become then.

Jamie met her outside the hospital that morning. He'd taken an overnight coach and walked from the station in the rain. Without a coat, being Jamie. His light blue hoodie was soaked to navy on the head and shoulders, and he looked pale. He stank of fags when she hugged him, although Louise didn't say anything about that; he knew her feelings on the subject. It should have been enough of a warning seeing the patients out in the bay where he was waiting for her, some in wheelchairs, others steadying themselves against the poles of their drips, all determined to smoke on to the last.

'Handsome Harry,' she said, giving him another squeeze. It was hard not to cry. Jamie asked her what she was like and patted her on the back so that he could step away. She could have sworn he'd grown.

Louise led him up to the children's ward. He was surprised at that; she thought she'd told him, with Holly only being thirteen. As he followed her directions to rub his hands with Sanigel from the dispenser at the door, she saw Jamie clock the little boy walk past with no hair or eyebrows. Liam.

'There's always someone worse off than you,' she whispered.

'Stuff reeks,' Jamie complained, holding his disinfected hands away from himself.

She'd warned him about Holly still being on medication for the pain, and how it could make her slow, but she was awake when they got to her, watching TV. It made Louise's eyes fill to see the smile Holly gave her brother as he loped to her bed, even though she squawked, 'Mind me leg!' when he dropped to cover her with a clumsy hug. She hadn't shown that much life for months. Jamie pulled up the chair by the bed and had a good look around, then back at Holly, riding the awkwardness, taking in the pinned casts that stopped her moving.

'Doesn't she look great?' said Louise. This made the two of them burst out laughing, for some reason. It was the way they were together, always had been. The laughter hurt her heart, with the strange pleasure of pressing on an old bruise.

'I knew you'd do her good,' she said, giving up trying to understand what was so funny. Anything set the two of them off, she knew.

Jamie nodded up at the telly on its ceiling bracket.

'Nice,' he said. Holly pointed to the bedside table and said, in just the same way, 'Nicer.' Their voices were solemn, which was part of the joke, but they were trying not to laugh. On the wall behind Holly's head was a framed print of a seaside scene: the striped backs of two deckchairs and a flag-topped sandcastle in pale, ice-cream colours.

'That's nice,' Louise offered. A look pinballed between Jamie and Holly, exploding both back into laughter.

'Don't,' Holly begged, tears on her cheeks, 'I've got to wee. Tell him, Mum.'

'It's not my fault!' said Jamie, delighted. But this was no laughing matter, now that the catheter was out, as Louise told him.

With him there, at least they didn't need to get hold of a nurse to struggle Holly into the wheelchair that waited by the bed. Holly didn't want Jamie to push it, though, as Louise suggested; she was indignant at the thought of her brother taking her to the toilet. When Louise got her into the cubicle she left her on her own, waiting for her resentful call of 'Finished'. Since the accident, Holly was more volatile about her privacy than she'd ever been. During the weeks at the hospital, Louise had learned that even the pleasure she took in brushing Holly's hair or smoothing a clean sleep T-shirt made her writhe and protest, as if intimate contact with her was a poisonous irritant. Now she restrained herself to basic help, although it was a daily battle of self-discipline. She could have crushed her with love, eaten her up with hugs and kisses, the way you wanted to eat babies.

When Louise wheeled Holly back, she asked to be left in the chair. Jamie was working his way through a packet of Nice biscuits he'd found on the bedside table. She saw that they would be okay without her for a few hours. In fact, they would enjoy it. She asked Jamie if she could have a word and nodded him out of his chair.

'What is it?' Holly wanted to know beadily, but Louise took him all the way to the nurse's station, out of earshot.

'Don't let her have your phone,' she told him.

She could see the surprise hit his face, but she knew Holly would try it on. Only a couple of days after she was out of intensive care, Louise had caught her, woozy from the drugs and with half her body in traction, trying to fumble the phone out of Louise's bag on the bed where she had left it on a trip to the coffee machine. To call *him*, of course. It was like getting her off smack. Since then, Louise had been careful. It was a mercy that Holly's body was healing, but there was still a battle to be fought, which was why she was particularly keen to talk to Kamila.

Jamie seemed to accept her command about not letting his sister near his phone. He'd always said that Louise could have gone to the police, with Holly's age and what that man had done—Louise could never bring herself to think he had a name—but she couldn't see the point if Holly still wanted to be with him. Holly might be underage but she'd never cooperate in any way, and it would just turn her further against her, if that was possible. And nearer to him, probably. Thinking about it, Louise grabbed at the corner of a larger understanding, that loving *him* was a way of hating Louise. Holly was too young to know that. Some people stayed too young the whole of their whole lives.

It was a beautiful day now, hot for early spring, the rain steaming off the roads and pavements as Louise drove herself back from the hospital. She'd told Jamie that she'd come back for him. It was ridiculous, really, not talking to Kamila on her mobile, but on the one occasion they'd tried it before, when Holly's consultant had rearranged an appointment at the last minute and she and Kamila ended up having a session with Louise sitting in the hospital car park, Kamila had found it hard to make contact. It made sense, that being in the house and calling from the phone that Mum had used for so many years allowed Kamila access to the vibrations she needed to do her work. Still, it was an unusual time for their call. Kamila preferred to work in the evenings, even late into the night; she said contact was always clearer the closer the material world was to sleep. But she had been firm that the only time possible today was early afternoon, between one and three.

The house felt empty when Louise opened the back door, which usually meant Patrick was asleep. Checking the momentum that followed the shove of effort needed to budge the misaligned wood, she nearly ran into a large cube in the middle of the kitchen floor, swaddled in bubble wrap and packing tape. The invoice papers stuck to the top of it told her that it was a dishwasher, and that Mia had signed for the delivery before she left for London. Stepping around it, Louise made herself a cup of tea and moved into the hall. She was in good time.

'This is Kamila.'

It was the way Kamila always answered, her accent crystalline and precise, her voice young, but today she sounded a little breathless, as though she'd had to hurry to pick up the phone. Just as they were about to get going properly, she excused herself—'Excuse me, Louise, I am so sorry'—and muffled the phone to have an unflustered yet still disconcerting exchange in her own language with someone else in the room. It was possible that she was asking them to leave. A child, perhaps? Louise had never considered where Kamila might live, or in what circumstances; the immateriality of her voice made it easy to think that, like the voices she was attuned to, she inhabited the ether. Forced to imagine her at all, Louise envisaged a kind of greeting-card sprite, inhabiting a pastel glade that owed nothing to nature.

Kamila's voice returned, in the usual brightly lulling tones. 'We are ready to begin. What questions do you have today, Louise?'

It was always such a relief, talking to her. Louise quickly got on to Jamie, and what she'd said to him about not letting Holly have his mobile, and her worry about Holly trying to run off again with that bastard the minute they were back in Leeds. As she always did, Kamila asked her to close her eyes, and then what colours she saw.

'Blue.'

'Light blue or dark?'

'Darkish. Not really dark. Sort of a royal blue, if you know what I mean.'

Kamila maintained her silence.

'Like the colour of school uniforms. Holly's school jumper, at their old school. The primary they both went to.'

'She is going back to school soon?'

'Not soon, but I've spoken to them. Probably not till after the summer holidays now.'

Another silence. 'I can feel the colours changing,' said Kamila.

Louise saw the veil of blue lighten. 'It's more yellow.'

'Yes, yellow. She's here with us. Sara. She wants you to know she loves you.'

'I love her too.'

'She knows this.'

However many times Louise heard it, it always made her cry.

It was a good session, the contact clearer than they'd had in weeks. At the end of the hour, after they'd arranged their next conversation, Louise wished Kamila a nice evening.

'I hope so,' she said. 'My boyfriend is taking me to the Bon Jovi concert!'

She sounded excited. 'Oh, well, have a lovely time,' said Louise. She forgave Kamila this small transgression into her private life, although she hoped it was a one-off. After Mum's communication, nothing was going to tarnish her good mood. It made all the difference in the world to her, to be so close at last.

For A Special Daughter
With Loving Thoughts on Your Birthday

To Louise,

On your special day
This comes to say
How much you're *cherished*
And how much *pride* is felt
Having a daughter
As *special* as you.

Lots of love from Mum and Patrick. xx oo

*Ps. Hope you can buy yourself
something nice with enclosed!*

WITH LOUISE'S DEPARTURE finally imminent, Mia was finding it hard to make any kind of social effort, or to pretend that her presence was anything but a nuisance. She was getting messier, for one thing. Each evening, Mia made collections of the objects Louise left around the house during the day and piled them neatly outside her door: reading glasses, mobile, cardigans, used tissues, puzzle magazines. She couldn't quite bring herself to include the dirtied mugs and plates that Louise and her son left scattered around, so she stacked these significantly short of the recently acquired dishwasher, trusting the message was clear.

As with any domestic matter, when Mia had spoken to Patrick about ordering the dishwasher, she may as well have been tweaking his earlobes or performing some similar act of low-level, meaningless provocation, which he manfully refused to rise to. After a few similar interchanges, Mia decided to take his irritated forbearance as a sanction for all aspects of her improvements scheme. From then on, when she needed Patrick's signature, she just presented the form or document without the aggravation of an explanation. He always signed. Mia had been slightly surprised, herself, that the bank had been willing to give him such a chunky loan for the kitchen renovation, but the house was worth a lot. 'Owner occupier' she had ticked on Patrick's behalf, when given the option on the forms. As for the credit cards, since she tended to use them over the phone, she didn't even need to trouble Patrick for a signature.

The dishwasher was a boon, and when the building foreman, Andy, came to talk to Mia about the work, he reassured her that they could leave it where it was for most of the duration. 'No problem' seemed to be his motto, dismissively tapping the surfaces and cabinets soon to be ripped out and replaced, breezily consigning them to history. It was nice to have a burst of energy in the house. Patrick had been ill; not seriously, but his mornings were starting towards lunchtime and he had a new cough in his repertoire that came in harsh volleys he had to suspend speaking or moving to withstand. Since the cough also troubled him at night, Mia had moved out again, not back to the den, but to one of the disused bedrooms at the end of the top corridor. Andy had said it would be no problem to install a new radiator in there, and that his crew could do it before they got going on the kitchen. He was as good as his word. Mia cleaned the room comprehensively, painted it in a week's worth of evenings, and had a new bed delivered, charged to one of the new cards. If Patrick had bothered to ask about the scheme, she would have offered her justification that he needed a guest room for all the visitors they seemed to be having, now that Louise occupied the spare room proper. He didn't ask.

Even after one night, Mia thought of the room as her own. Its deep casement looked over the back of the house, to the sea. Although she rarely looked out of the window, she cherished the idea of it. She Instagrammed a phone shot of the view. After all that rain, the weather had turned freakishly warm, with steady sun gilding unseasonably decorous waves.

Just before eight on the builders' first day, Mia was at the door to welcome them, hopeful that Patrick wouldn't be disturbed, given his habitual deep sleep and the fact that his bedroom sat over the opposite side of the house. At the sight of the van she felt nervously excited, as though complicit in a small crime. She offered cups of tea, but Andy and his assembly of silent, fleece-wearing men were already sipping from lidded paper cups of their own. She left them to it. Less than five minutes later, Louise barged her bedroom door so hard that the knob dented the new paintwork.

'What's going on?'

Mia looked up from her laptop, where she was trying to source a cheap version of shelving she had admired on the walls of a converted Belgian orphanage in *ELLE Decoration*.

'They're working on the kitchen.'

Louise's breath came deeply, wheezing. 'Working?'

Not for the first time, Mia was tempted to announce her engagement.

'It should have been ripped out twenty years ago. It's totally had it.' From downstairs, a woody wrenching underlined Mia's point. Louise took a step back, hanging on to the door, banjaxed. Mia's presence on the night of Holly's accident had led her to believe that Mia was an ally, an article of good faith she still clung to in spite of the deterioration of Mia's tone.

'Does Nigel know?'

'Why would he?'

Mia decided to ring him first. She didn't think there was much chance of Nigel backing Louise against her. But his mobile and his work number both went straight to voicemail. Louise was probably down the corridor, blocking the lines. Mia hovered in her doorway and listened. Louise was talking, all right, but she was talking to Jamie; Mia could hear his responses, measured and brief against his mother's flow of agitation. He wasn't a talker; that seemed to run in the family. Patrick talked for all of them. Had that been true for Sara as well? Mia dismissed the question. Louise's ridiculous communion with the spirit world was a Pandora's box left temptingly open. She refused to succumb to curiosity: it would mean Louise had won something. If she could just hang on for a few more days, Louise would be gone and Mia could have everything she wanted.

Self-consciously casual, Mia left her room. Patrick's bedroom door was still closed, its scuffed wood incommunicative. Increasingly, when she'd left him for any length of time, the thought came to her: what if he were dead? Her pulse tripped as she opened the door. Patrick, on the side of the bed, paused in putting on his socks. His feet dangled a bathetic few centimetres from the floor, one socked, the other naked and veined. Unusually, Mia went to him and dropped a kiss on his head. He held her to him, warm and animal with his recent sleep. Alive, then.

'You're the world to me, darling girl.'

This meant it was going to be one of his good days; the builders couldn't have woken him. He looked at her, up and down. Mia had come to understand what the phrase 'drinking in' meant as a way of looking—the thirsty progress of Patrick's eyes, relieving a basic need.

'You're man's answer to God,' he said. 'You're all there is.' The hairs that poked from his unbuttoned pyjama top were grey and wiry. She settled them with her palm as a fusillade of coughing overtook him. If he died and they weren't married, she'd be left with nothing. She didn't want much, she really didn't.

'I'll bring your tea.'

Mia had moved the kettle, toaster and relevant supplies into Patrick's study. While she was jiggling toast free from the ejecting mechanism, Jamie sidled round the door. Talking to her didn't come easily, Mia saw; even the rims of his ears were a hot red. For the first time, she saw a resemblance to Nigel. He was Jamie's uncle, after all.

'Mum's a bit upset.'

Mia waited for Jamie to say more, but that seemed to be as much as he could muster. She put the slices on to the plate and cymballed her palms free of crumbs.

'When isn't she upset?'

Eyes widening with surprise, Jamie grinned. Mia smiled back.

'It's just—anything to do with her mum, you know. It upsets her.'

'What does the kitchen have to do with her mum?'

He shrugged, on the spot.

'Would you like some toast? Sorry, I should have thought . . .'

He considered the offer as though it gave him pain.

'Go on, then.'

Mia knew from her years in Newcastle that northern people always met hospitable gestures as though they were doing you a favour. She proffered Jamie the plate and put in another couple of slices for Patrick as Jamie mortared cold chippings of butter on to his toast. Despite the sunshine outside, the study remained inhospitably cool.

'I know it's a bit inconvenient, but it'll only be a couple of weeks. It's not like they're tearing the place down—it's a few units, for God's sake.'

Jamie stood, and munched.

'Nothing to do with me, is it.'

Thank God for that. She made him a coffee along with Patrick's. He blushed again when he took it. It wasn't a particular blush, she could see; he was just shy.

'I'm off soon.'

Like a tap with a slow drip, Jamie's speech seemed to take a while to gather in him before it could be expressed.

'Into t'army. Basic training, like.'

'Your mum hadn't said,' said Mia, as though she and Louise chatted about these things.

'She dun't know.'

Mia was surprised by his confiding in her. But who else did he have to tell, apart from Patrick? Maybe he had told him already. A couple of times she had been surprised to find the two of them in apparently easy conversation about football. They had that in common, as well as cricket, racing, snooker and Formula One. Since Jamie's arrival, Patrick had been enticed to watch more of these than ever on the TV in the den, at all hours.

Jamie slurped coffee. 'I'll tell her, like. Working up to it. She'll feel better about stuff once she's got Holly from the hospital.'

Mia picked up the breakfast things for Patrick, leaving Jamie to it. She half-expected to see Louise in the hall as she passed through, receiving confidences from the Other Side, but there was no sign of her. As Mia reached the stairs, the phone rang baldly. Backtracking, she picked it up and answered. There was a small, charged hesitation before an elderly woman's voice said, 'Oh, hello, I was hoping to speak with Patrick.' The voice was lush, burred with nicotine. Mia suppressed a small surge of fright.

'Who shall I say is calling?'

'Dodie Shad.'

Not Sara then, of course not. Mia asked the woman to hold the line. Phone calls for Patrick were rare enough for her to feel curious and slightly excited on his behalf. When he heard who it was, he gave a quavering, matter-of-fact sigh and stumped downstairs, as though people were beleaguering him by phone every minute of the day. Mia lingered on the landing.

'Dodie.'

Patrick's hand stole to his forelock, and he instantly became more robust, even dashing. She couldn't infer much of the conversation, as Dodie appeared to be doing most of the talking. 'Cradle-snatching,' Patrick agreed at one point, which Mia assumed alluded to her. The conversation lasted for less than five minutes. Replacing the receiver, Patrick headed for his study without turning back. She had to scuttle after him with the cooling coffee and cold toast. He received them neutrally and took them to his desk. Jamie had cleared out, leaving his mug neatly on his empty plate, by the kettle.

'So?'

Patrick glared. 'Is there any marmalade?'

She brought it for him. Through the crunching, Patrick told Mia that Dodie and her husband, Lucas, would be staying the following night, on their way to a literary event in Padstow. This was something they had done occasionally when Sara was alive, although not for a number of years. Mia stared at him as he dropped a crust to his plate. At some point she had imagined entertaining in the house, drifting from one streamlined surface to the other as she assembled an effortless meal, sharing a bottle of champagne with her guests. But now was definitely not that point.

'We don't have a kitchen!'

'We'll go out. They'll pay, since we're putting them up. Although Lucas can be tight as fucking *arseholes*.'

Mia made a booking for a bistro in Newquay. She found it online when the restaurant Patrick mentioned as the place he and Sara always went to with Dodie and Lucas turned out to have gone bust in 2003. On the assumption the Shads shared Patrick's conservatism, she chose somewhere she hoped would be similar in atmosphere and menu to their extinct regular, and booked a table for four. She bought gin and lemons and minibar cans of tonic, and proper whisky instead of Patrick's own-brand stuff, hiding it among the cereal packets so that he wouldn't start the bottle before the visitors arrived. She stowed a bag of ice cubes in the stranded freezer. As a final gesture, she picked the tulips and grape hyacinths that bloomed randomly in the garden and arranged them in vases. Opening the windows of the damp drawing room to the welcome spring heat, Mia felt her keenest pleasure: life as magazine shoot. *Mia likes to brighten the eighteenth-century drawing room with flowers from the garden.* She Instagrammed a shot of the flowers, her face a blur behind them.

The next day, the Shads arrived nearly two hours before they were expected, while Patrick was having his study-based nap.

Louise and Jamie had left for the hospital, and in any case were neither expected nor asked to play any part in the socialising. Mia answered the door.

'Wonderful journey, we just cruised straight through, didn't even stop for a pee!' announced Dodie, foursquare on the doorstep. She was a tall woman, extravagantly layered against any defining assessment of her large body. Clumped mascara framed her sentimental blue eyes, which blinked through a girlish ash-blonde fringe, so that the top of her face in no way corresponded to the swags and puckerings of age further down. She offered a warm hand, armoured with rings.

'You must be Mia.'

Mia smiled and withstood the frank scrutiny of both Shads. Lucas, smaller than his wife, stepped out from behind her, armed with a bottle that he forced into Mia's hands as he lunged in for a double kiss. He was dapper, smoothly bald. Mia hadn't been prepared for a friend of Patrick's to be black. (His Wiki entry said a lot about a small magazine, and jazz; she had skimmed it without looking up any images.)

'Where is the old bugger?'

Mia told them that Patrick was working, and apologised about the kitchen, where drilling whined through the walls. While Lucas went to find Patrick, she led Dodie upstairs with their bags: Mia had decamped back to Patrick's bedroom to make way for their guests.

'Absolutely desperate for a pee, we were so determined not to stop,' said Dodie, disappearing into the bathroom on the way. Mia carried the bags on into the bedroom for her. They were of unremarkable quality, she assessed, neither the cheapest nor shabby with age. Going by these as well as their car, the Shads weren't rich, but they didn't look to be strapped, either. Dodie took so long in the bathroom that Mia went back downstairs, where Patrick was already shuffling around in search of a drink.

'House is in a bloody uproar,' he complained to Lucas, who sat in the spare chair, legs urbanely crossed to reveal burgundy socks and skinny, hairless shins. Mia intercepted the Basics whisky bottle and asked Lucas what he would really like.

By the time of their dinner reservation, everyone except Mia had been drinking for hours. Although Lucas showed no signs of being affected by the gin and tonics that kept pace with Patrick's scotches, Dodie was slurring her words and repeating herself, with an increasingly irritating habit of buttonholing Mia every time the conversation between the two men became interesting. Fortunately, the older woman seemed to be seeking an outlet for monologue rather than an actual conversation, so after a couple of frustrating interchanges, Mia was able to tune her out and listen to the men. She relished the opportunity to eavesdrop on Patrick, performing the way he had on the phone to Dodie, all frailty banished. He was exactly the way she had imagined he might be before she met him.

It took some chivvying to get the uproarious trio of them moving in time for dinner. The Shads, supported by Patrick, were adamant that there was no point paying for a taxi when their perfectly good car was parked outside. When Mia protested that Lucas was over the limit, he flourished his car keys and suggested that she drive. She decided to take Dodie's breezy assurances about the scope of their insurance coverage at face value.

'What a shame we couldn't get into the old place,' sighed Dodie, as Mia parked. Mia had twice explained to the Shads, as well as Patrick, that the old place was defunct.

'Never liked it!' said Patrick. 'Manager was a cunt. Came from Guildford and wore a fucking beret.'

Mia was relieved when the waiter settled them at a back table, away from draughts, as Dodie demanded, and with sufficient space around them to avoid disruption to the rest of the tamer and mainly younger clientele. Did old people really speak more loudly because they were deaf, Mia wondered, or just because they had the kind of voices no one had any more? Dodie had imparted early in her monologue that she had trained as an actress in the 1960s.

'Julie Christie was in my year at RADA.'

Mia hadn't asked her who Julie Christie was. She could look it up later.

Lucas ignored the menu being placed in front of him and buttonholed the waiter for a bottle of house red. Dodie, once she had retrieved her reading glasses from the chain where they rested on her mounded bosom, compensated by taking a beady interest in her own menu's contents. She read most of it out loud, relishing a couple of spelling mistakes and deploring a comprehensive lack of accents and circumflexes.

'Are you up to the entrecôte, Paddy?' Dodie asked. 'Or entre-*coat*, as I suppose it's prounounced . . . it was always your favourite at the other place.'

'You know what I like,' Patrick told Mia, as uninterested as Lucas in the prospect of food.

Dodie, with a practised shoulder turn, appealed to the gallery. 'What's a "steak-cut chip" when it's at home?'

'At least they're not "fries".'

Mia was aware that Lucas was staring at her as he spoke. She smiled at him politely. He batted Patrick.

'You old dog, look at her!'

When the wine came ('About bloody time,' said Patrick, as Lucas dismissed the waiter's offer of a taste and indicated that his glass should be filled immediately), Dodie insisted on a toast.

'To Mia, and new beginnings.'

Mia accepted the tribute; Patrick had told them, then, about the proposal. (She couldn't properly call it an engagement, with no ring to show for it.) Dodie hoisted her glass again, shushing the men.

'And to dear Sara, and times past.'

Her voice faltered, eyes swimming. Patrick was already lifting his own glass to drink, so that Lucas, attempting to slosh his glass against Patrick's for the second toast, instead tipped wine on to the tablecloth. The waiter came and blotted a folded napkin over the purple stain.

'What's a steak-cut chip?' Dodie asked him, with a flirtatious shift in tone. The waiter struggled to explain.

'It's just a chip then, that you eat with steak,' she declared, projecting to the room with the confidence of delivering a killing bon mot. The waiter agreed, flicking a look at Mia that appealed both to their similar age and Mia's implied role as carer. She was surprised to intercept an equally complicit eye roll from Patrick, uniting himself with her against Dodie. She lengthened the smile she had produced for the waiter to include him, surprised. This was a new alliance between them. Or was it? Seeing Patrick turn back to Lucas, her faint surge of affection ebbed. It hadn't been meant for her, that look, just aimed at the hole that she filled. *Dear Sara and times past.* Don't look in the box, she admonished herself. Deal, or no deal. Sara was only a person, like any other, and what do people matter?

Mia decided she'd better stop drinking. The food arrived. She had ordered fish for Patrick, knowing steak was beyond his teeth. The men progressed to their second bottle of wine, but Dodie, belatedly recognising her own limit, left her glass untouched. From time to time, she and Lucas looked at each other and smiled.

You never know what really goes on inside a marriage, babe. When her dad had said this to her, as a teenager, Mia had assumed that it was meant to dismiss mysteries of sex too uncomfortable to discuss between a father and daughter, particularly the irreconcilable mysteries both of sex between her parents and sex between her father and his new girlfriend. It seemed, though, that sex might be the least of it.

'Oh no, I can't eat this.'

Dodie was giving her chicken the same critical attention she had beamed on the menu.

'It's full of something. I simply can't eat it.'

Lucas's face jumped into loyal dismay. 'No good?'

'Tarragon.'

'Tell the man!'

The waiter was forbearing. Presently, Dodie was brought a plain grilled chicken breast, which she pronounced dry, incorporating a shrug of martyred forbearance into the thorough chewing of each morsel. While she finished it, Dodie resumed an earlier monologue about the festival in Padstow where Lucas was scheduled to speak, which seemed largely to concern a historical grudge with the organiser, whom she referred to as Cruella de Vil. Mia drifted in and out, thinking about the unit handles for the kitchen. Was brushed steel really the best option, or verging on outdated? Perhaps tongue-and-groove might have been better for the units themselves. A contemporary kitchen might just look plain wrong. Anyway, she consoled herself, whatever she did and whatever Louise thought about it, it was bound to be an improvement.

'. . . loved Paddy to have come along, but Sara absolutely forbade it, of course.'

Mia tuned in. 'Sorry?'

'Sara. Cruella would have adored Paddy to make an appearance, but he could never get permission from home, could you Paddy?'

Patrick turned his attention from his wine glass to Dodie.

'Padstow,' she reminded him. 'Sara wasn't keen.'

'Not my sort of thing.' He pushed his plate away, conclusively. 'Anyway, she liked having me at home.'

And now Mia witnessed a marital look between the Shads, surprisingly acute despite its buffer of alcohol. *This one again*, it said. *Yeah, right.*

'You could go with Lucas, check it out,' Mia suggested, but Patrick was too soaked in booze to absorb anything else that night.

He hadn't been wrong about the bill. Lucas and Dodie's failure to display the merest flicker of acknowledgement when the waiter placed the leatherette wallet on the table suggested a prior agreement between them to ignore it. The card Mia took out to pay was Patrick's, although she punched in the PIN.

In the car on the way home, Dodie finally lapsed into queasy silence beside Mia as she drove, allowing her to digest the evening. *She liked having me at home.* The look shared by the Shads during the Padstow conversation either meant that they thought Sara's behaviour, or Patrick's defence of it, was bizarre. Given Louise, and the condition of the house, it wouldn't be surprising if Sara had been a bit of a fruit loop. She had certainly been nothing like Mia, whatever Louise's psychic claimed. As far as Mia was concerned, Patrick was welcome to go to Padstow any time he liked. She'd drive him there herself.

Beside her, Dodie belched richly.

'Of course she stopped him—stopped him writing,' she slurred, as though Mia had already put a question to her. 'Lucas says he'll never forgive her for that.'

'Stopped him? Sara?'

Dodie gathered her layers around her, as though this indiscretion had accidentally tumbled from her clothing.

'Not my place to say, darling.'

'But how could she have stopped him—'

'Hush. Or you'll bring down the wrath . . .'

Dodie jerked her head at the back seat, where Lucas and Patrick dozed. A trailing snore came from one of them.

'The wrath is mighty, when it descends, I'm sure you know . . .'

'They can't hear you, they're completely out of it.' Mia glanced at Dodie, deciding how to play it. 'He said she liked having him at home. Wasn't—'

Wasn't that so he could write, she was about to say, but Dodie leaped in. 'I'm not sure she did, quite honestly. Dog in the manger, darling.'

'I don't know what that means,' Mia told her.

Authoritative, Dodie shook out a layer.

'She was a tricky one, Sara. Lovely, of course. But hard to fathom sometimes. Not like me—I'm an open book! What you see is what you get, absolute heart on sleeve. I was fond of her—don't get me wrong . . . But Paddy. Well. Tell it not in Gath, but I'm not sure she wanted him, really. *Him*. But she certainly didn't want anyone else to have him.'

For the rest of the journey Dodie remained silent, misty eyes on the black road being gulped by the full beam of the headlights. When they arrived at the house, Mia had to wake Lucas and Patrick to help them both, stumbling around the obstacle of Louise's parked car, inside. Dodie waited by the front door. With an air of long practice, she deftly took some of Lucas's weight, while hooking her free hand on Mia's sleeve.

'You do know what you're doing, dear, don't you?'

At first Mia thought Dodie meant getting Patrick up to bed. Then she realised; she meant marrying him.

'I think so,' Mia said, disengaging herself from Dodie and steering Patrick to the stairs.

You never know what really goes on inside a marriage. Sitting on the bed, it took Patrick the same time to toe his shoes off from the back, blundering, pissed, as it did for her to get undressed and hang up her clothes. What was she doing? He was a million years old. *Him.* The way Dodie had said that, it was as though she had fancied Patrick, once upon a time. Was that what had happened, she'd had a go, and Sara had seen her off? It seemed incredible now, listening to Patrick coughing volcanically all the time she was brushing her teeth. He was still coughing when she came back into the bedroom, struggling at his pyjama buttons. Really, she should fetch him a glass of water. Slipping first under the duvet, Mia decided to let him wait until he woke in the night with his drinker's thirst. Or, if he was desperate enough, he could go and get one now. There was no point giving in to him; he had to learn to do things for himself. She wasn't Sara.

Your agent's office phoned. An assistant called Jay or Jake?? (sounds very young!) returning your call to Peter, says sorry it's been so long. It's a no from radio people.

Sorry about this morning. Maybe it's my age. But talking about things seems completely pointless as far as I'm concerned.

Gone to shops. Sx

Ps. Don't touch ham, it's for tonight.

SOPHIE HAD BEEN right in insisting that a pool for the boys was a deal-breaker; when they arrived at the country-house hotel after another tortuously long drive from Surrey, the rain was torrential. The forecasts for their week away were dismal. Fortunately, only Nigel seemed cowed by the prospect.

'Cornwall,' said Sophie, with a tolerant, proprietary air, snapping up her umbrella and chivvying the dazed boys across the teeming gap from car to lobby. The weather wasn't going to put her off, Nigel could see. Despite her first visit being ambushed by the melodrama of Holly's accident, the second-home bit had never left Sophie's teeth. Behind the scenes, she had been steadily amassing information and constructing Pinterest boards. Critically galvanised by some Norfolk renovation shots circulated at a recent dinner party, Nigel suspected that Sophie had pushed for this trip mainly because she no longer trusted him to finesse matters with Patrick and Louise without her supervision. And it was true; he'd been avoiding the necessary conversation for so long that, in some unthinkable benchmark of procrastination, Patrick's solicitor had actually started to call him. Since Nigel never procrastinated, he knew the disposition of the house must be worrying him at some profoundly unreachable level. Whether it was Patrick or Louise he was more fearful of confronting, it was hard to say, but with Holly recovered, there was no longer any excuse not to tackle Louise.

'Isn't it called something?' Sophie asked, during the journey. Nigel told her he'd only ever known it as 'The House'. Its legal address was 6 Hill Path; 'Hill Path House' made you sound like you were trying out dentures, or ordering Thai food. Perhaps there had been a name, historically, and Patrick had got rid of it. He had been very against history, once. When Nigel declared it to be his favourite subject at school he remembered Patrick condemning the way it was taught, along with television, books, sport and the pop charts, as a cultural opiate. Military history particularly got his goat: 'a wet-dream of Britannia', apparently.

'We can always think of a name,' Sophie had said.

Despite being welded to their DVD players in the back of the car, as before the boys had nodded off for the last hour or so of the journey, which meant that by the time they arrived at the hotel they were bouncing off the walls instead of winding down sufficiently to allow their parents the adult dinner with them asleep at the end of the baby monitor Nigel had been wistfully anticipating. Since they would all be sharing a family room, he had already resigned himself to the lack of hotel sex; the prospect of a proper meal and an overpriced bottle of wine had been his small comfort. But Sophie ended up ordering grey room-service hamburgers, which they all ate crowded on the big bed while watching a digital repeat of *Have I Got News For You*, the only programme they could find not wildly unsuitable for the boys, given the lateness of the hour and their enthusiasm for the giant screen. Olly asked so many questions in his struggle to understand that Nigel snapped at him and Sophie got annoyed at him snapping. In the ensuing spat, Nigel was forced to play the working-all-week card.

Finally, but only after Albie had trapped his fingers in the hinge of the wardrobe Olly was repeatedly slamming and wailed himself to sleep in the aftermath, the boys were out for the count. Nigel and Sophie slept turned away from each other until Albie woke in the early hours, disorientated and panicking, and Sophie gathered him in. Olly crept into the bed at his usual time, before six, and Nigel's remaining sleep was so cramped and fitful that finally he got up, pulled on his kit and ran a three-mile circuit around the sodden hotel grounds. Throughout, he could feel his neck pinching from the tension of his nighttime position. He wasn't looking forward to the day.

After breakfast (the boys, but not Nigel, were allowed Coco Pops), they set off to the house. Nigel had called Louise to warn her of their arrival, but not that he wanted to speak to her in particular. Sophie briefly rehearsed the pitch with him in the car.

Mia, answering the door, was as pristine as ever, the jeans as snug. As she led them through the markedly tidier hall, Sophie pulled a face of pantomime prurience behind her back and Nigel felt a twinge of irritation at this claim on his marital loyalty. He had, of course, told her about the wedding plans, with an admonition not to let them slip to Louise.

'Patrick's asleep,' Mia told them. This was surprising, given the full-blooded hammerings and drillings from the direction of the kitchen. 'Your sister's in the dining room.'

Louise was perched on one of the frail chairs, drinking coffee, her hands slack around the mug. Nigel registered his wife's assimilation of all the facts of Louise's appearance: size, clothes, damaged pallor. They had never met before, although Louise had been dutifully invited to their wedding, and had tactfully declined to attend, as Nigel had secretly hoped. Seamlessly Sophie stepped in, and air-kissed.

'You must be Louise—how lovely to meet you.'

Louise, laughing in nervous surprise at Sophie's metropolitan second pass, botched the greeting. She moved on to Nigel, relieved to fuss the boys.

'Bless them. Look at his hair! Haven't you got lovely hair?' Albie, blankly accustomed to this response to his crown of ringlets, said nothing. Nigel was privately waiting for the day it was all cut off. He could have had hair like that once, if it had been allowed.

'Mum's hair,' said Louise.

'Wasted on a boy!' laughed Sophie, as always.

'And you're a big boy,' Louise said to Olly. 'How old are you now?'

Olly retreated behind his mother.

'Oliver,' Nigel warned.

'Six,' said Sophie.

'Six!' Louise exclaimed. A silence followed.

'How's Holly doing?' Sophie asked. At this, Louise buckled and began to sob, apologising at the same time. Albie and Olly stared. They had never seen an adult cry before. Sophie, saying something about a glass of water, shot a look to Nigel that commanded him to get the boys out of the room. Relieved by this division of labour, he brightly suggested they have an explore. He hadn't realised Holly was still such a source of distress, although Louise had always been prone to what their mother called piping her eye.

'Look at all those books!' he enthused, out in the corridor. It was too wet to go into the garden, and he knew better than to take them upstairs if Patrick was sleeping.

'Dis library?' asked Albie, optimistically. He associated the library with juice and a biscuit. Olly wanted to know when they could go swimming at the hotel. Soon, Nigel promised. Struggling, he suggested they try counting all the books on the shelf. While he was doing this, alone, because Olly refused and Albie was too small to get beyond ten, his nephew appeared. He was there at the foot of the stairs when Nigel turned round, tall and alarming. Nigel jumped slightly.

'All right?' said the boy. Young man. Jamie, wasn't it? Although he was fully dressed, his huge, hairy feet were bare. A large hollow black disc distended the lobe of one ear, and his forearms were dense with hostile-looking tattoos.

The boys stared as Nigel introduced them to their 'cousin Jamie'. Jamie smiled and passed them, and Nigel saw Olly trying to make some connection with this alien creature and the adored den-building, cello-playing Big Cousins on Sophie's side.

'Was the other one a cousin?' he asked.

He meant Mia. Nigel told him that she wasn't. The boys, alerted by the sound of the TV from the room Jamie had entered, trailed up the corridor after him. Nigel allowed them to follow. Olly wanted to know if they could get Cartoon Network.

'You can get anything.'

Jamie showed Olly the remote, bending to indicate the menu button with a bitten-nailed index finger. Nigel was surprised by the attentiveness of the gesture. Perhaps he was a nice enough kid. The three of them—small, medium and large—gathered on the sofa as Jamie found *Scooby-Doo.*

'All right?'

Olly nodded, settling in the cushions as Albie slotted his fingers in his mouth and trustingly cuddled up to his new relative. In the middle, Jamie gave a loose sigh, his head the only part of him angled above the horizontal.

Nigel left the three of them to it and went upstairs to see if he could happen on Mia. There was no doubt that the house was looking much better. He doubted Sophie would be giving Mia much credit for that.

'Patrick.'

There he stood on the landing, dressed, his atmosphere wholly unstirred by Nigel's appearance. Like the house, Patrick looked sprucer. It was hard to say why; perhaps a matter of food stains?

'Haven't seen my specs, have you?'

'No,' said Nigel.

As usual, Nigel experienced the force of Patrick's personality as a tide swirling over a castle that only in that moment of catastrophe realised it was made of sand. Presumably Patrick had struck his mother like that, with added sex. And now Mia.

'They're in the bathroom!'

That was her, calling from the bedroom. Patrick's bedroom. His mother's bedroom, unless you listened to Louise's theory. That it had been separate bedrooms, possibly for years, as Mum endured her illness and Patrick refused to let her tell him and Louise about it. Mia's sleek head appeared from behind the door.

'You left them in the bathroom,' she said. 'But Dodie's in there, Patrick.'

'Why in Christ's name would I have left them in there?'

'Dodie, gosh,' Nigel said. This explained the extra car in the drive. Then, ingratiatingly, 'You appear to be running a guest-house.'

'Over my dead fucking body!'

Nigel recognised the symptoms of a pernicious hangover. Perhaps there would be a scene. Nigel knew Sophie wouldn't approve of this. Their argument last night had taken place behind the door of the hotel bathroom, so strongly did they both feel about exposing the boys to any of the less enjoyable emotions. There was also the swearing to consider. He followed Patrick downstairs, prepared to overtake. Patrick, though, seemed in no particular hurry.

'You see her son's fetched up on the fucking doorstep now?'

Sophie would definitely have views. Socially, she got a kick out of purveying his family, in contrast to her own, as outrageous; at a party he had once heard her allude to 'Nigel's secret chav origins', a word she had forbidden Olly to use when he brought it home from school. But Nigel suspected she might be finding this exoticism less adorable upon contact, which brought, after all, the possibility of contagion. Jamie's ear loop had alerted in Nigel a frisson of the forbidden, one of the myriad corrupters he had been programmed by Sophie to prevent the boys from encountering. In truth, he knew she would have balked at Cartoon Network, since most facets of English life after 1980 were out of bounds to their children. At least it was only Scooby effing Doo.

'He's only staying for a few days, Patrick.' This was Mia, swinging out from the bedroom, carrying a large tray. Nigel assimilated the dismaying lack of deference in her tone and all the intimacy it implied.

Patrick snorted, and continued downstairs. Nigel went back to help. Mia didn't fight him for the tray. He was relieved to see a single mug, a single toast-crumbed plate. Breakfast in bed for one. As if they weren't sharing a bed. They were getting married, for God's sake. He summoned several things he wanted to say, but none of them formed appropriately.

'We could all go out for lunch,' he proffered.

Mia looked taken aback by this suggestion, emanating nothing-to-do-with-her, although Nigel had been attempting to show consideration. Did he seem strange to her? He was the normal one, after all. Descending below them, Patrick's mane mocked him. If only he had more bloody hair.

'Lucas!'

The histrionic bellow from the bathroom stopped them all short. Above them, Dodie—a name invoked by his mother to which Nigel was now able to put an unexpected face—emerged. She braced herself against the doorframe, panting.

'I knew that wretched chicken was off. Darling, I'm really not sure I can face Padstow!'

'Oh God,' Mia said, from his shoulder. 'Chicken, my arse.' Which surprised, then pleased him. Before Nigel had a chance to respond, she had skipped back upstairs, asking Dodie, in the most solicitous tones, whether she could get her anything.

Downstairs, Patrick headed for his study. Sophie was still in the dining room, attentively inclined to Louise's monologue about Holly and her recovery, but as soon as she saw Nigel she pushed her chair back and said she should check the boys weren't up to mischief. The brief panic in Louise's eyes as Sophie abandoned the room acknowledged the strangeness of the two of them being alone together. Nigel knew he needed to launch in; Louise was already shuffling back her own chair.

'Louise—'

He sat down. Obediently, she followed suit. Feeling his chest tightening against the damp, he took out his inhaler, sprayed and inhaled deeply. Sophie was right. It was high time all this was sorted out.

Nigel first set out the terms of the will concerning the house. He had anticipated having to repeat himself to clarify Louise's muddy understanding, but she seemed to grasp what he was saying unusually well.

'So we own it between us?'

'Effectively. I think Patrick's accountant when they bought the place—it was the era of supertax and all that—must have been terrifically paranoid about them paying over the odds, so he encouraged them to put the house in Mum's name, along with all the rights.'

'Rights?'

'To his plays. Patrick must have been earning money hand over fist at that point.'

Louise slumped, hands inadequately guarding the spread of her belly. It was impossible to tell what she was thinking, or if she was thinking at all.

'It doesn't mean we have to do anything,' Nigel pointed out. 'In fact, I think the last thing we should do is anything hasty.'

'God knows what it's worth,' she said.

Although Nigel had already considered arranging a valuation, the same curiosity from Louise's mouth sounded distastefully venal.

'Well, that will be something to consider in the, er, fullness of time.'

Chair pushed back from the table, Louise contemplated her surprisingly small, shoeless feet, clad in sheer black tights or pop socks (she was wearing her usual leggings) with opaque caps obliterating the toes. She wriggled herself into a more erect position, as though chided to sit up straight.

'We could chuck Patrick out then. Out on the street.'

Once again, although the thought had formed readily enough, Nigel was repulsed by the prospect of sharing even that with her. Even worse was the oddly childish gurgle of laughter that accompanied Louise's suggestion, leading back somewhere he fastidiously refused to go.

'Not exactly,' he counselled. 'Not in his lifetime. Which is only as it should be.'

'What if he got married again?' she asked, skewering him. Had Mia told her, then?

'Well, that would be a different matter entirely. It would be hard for him to make a case, I suppose . . .'

Louise examined her feet again.

'Listen to me. Why would he get married again? Not that it matters . . .'

So Mia had said nothing. Good. Better not to muddy the water. In he went.

'I have a proposition—a suggestion.'

It unfolded just as he and Sophie had rehearsed. That they couldn't know how long Patrick had left to live, and that it was right and decent that they should allow him to live in the house as long as he wished. That, however, the house represented a substantial asset, and that Louise, Nigel imagined, could do with the money from the house right now. That Nigel was willing to advance her her share of the equity in return for the other half of the house, so that it was entirely his. That he and Sophie would start to do some work on the house with a view to using it as a second home, subject to suitable arrangements with Patrick. The money, for Louise, would be a life-transforming amount—enough for a new, bigger house in Leeds, as well as to set up Jamie and Holly properly when they needed it. This was something he really hoped she would think about.

As he spoke, the colour in Louise's face rose beneath her make-up. Her breathing always had a catch at the end of it, a remote cellophane crackle. Asthma like his, perhaps, or simply the effect of her weight. It had become more pronounced as his proposition developed.

'Nidge, I've got to tell you, this is—this just proves it. She wants me to stay.'

'Holly?'

This seemed unlikely. And she couldn't mean Mia, surely.

'*Mum*. She's here. She's looking after us.'

Nigel quelled his urge to look round and complete Louise's sightline into the corner of the musty room. She was offering her hand across the table. He took it, in a reflex quasi-handshake. He felt, even more than confused, profoundly embarrassed.

'It's like she arranged it all.'

'I think you'll find it was the accountant—'

'All I want is to keep Holly safe. If I can stay here, if I can tell Patrick that's my right, I can keep her safe, can't I? Away from everything back home. That's all I want.'

She was squeezing hard on his hand. When Nigel looked up from the worn Turkish rug, his sister's tear-brimmed eyes were bright with unusual self-conviction.

'But what about the money?'

'Money isn't everything—Mum'd say the same, wouldn't she? Sometimes you have to trust in the universe. I've always believed that,' Louise said. 'Us getting the house, it's a sign. That's what Kamila said—*She wants you to stay*. This proves it.'

His violent flare of anger was almost immediately damped out by hopelessness. Nigel saw that Louise was as intractable to reason as she had been at eight, resisting his arguments against Father Christmas. When he had pointed out the price sticker that had been left on the box of his Scalextric, she had countered with a stubborn theory that your parents actually bought the presents from Father Christmas, maintaining that this only made more sense of the whole arrangement. Suddenly, Nigel longed to crawl under the table and rest. Perhaps the woolliness that he had ascribed to the combination of sleeplessness and humidity in fact signalled the beginning of a virus.

He flinched as Louise put the back of her hand against his clammy cheek. 'Nidge. Do you remember trampolines?'

It was a game they used to play on his bed, long before Patrick, or St Kit's, jumping as high as they could, her down abetting his up. He remembered the wiry groan of the mattress, their laughter, and their mother coming in to put a stop to their pleasure in the guise of alarm over damage they were doing to the bed. Legs had been slapped and as the eldest he had got the blame, although, to be fair, it had probably been his idea.

Louise squeezed his hand again. Her skin was hot. 'She's looking after us, Nidge. She always has.'

Above them, a heavy footfall thundered in the direction of the bathroom. Dodie. He realised it was high time to get the boys out of the house and into the pool.

That night, Nigel, pink-eyed with chlorine, debriefed Sophie over stringy hotel guinea fowl. The boys, duly exhausted by swimming, had been put to bed, the monitor displaying a flat green line of silent bars where it sat on the table between them in the fashionably gloomy dining room. Listening to his account of the conversation with Louise, Sophie agreed that all kinds of trouble might lie ahead, but she was far more sanguine than him, which helped. She always helped. What a woman she was. Louise though, Louise: it was hardly the poor bitch's fault, and it shouldn't come as a surprise, but as he said to Sophie, she was as mad as a box of fucking frogs.

21 Today

You've got the key of the door,
You've never been *21* before

Happy 21st Nigel,

With all our love,
Mum and Patrick xxxxxxxx

PS Travelling sounds wonderful.
Lucky you, wish we could get away!

PPS. Believe it or not, we've bought a new car!

On the day Holly was due to get back from hospital, Louise's excitement was tainted only by her nerves at confronting Patrick. She knew it would be all right, with Mum smiling down, but she also knew there was unpleasantness to face before everything was sorted. It was a relief at first that so much of the morning was taken up by the departure of the Shads, who had stayed an extra night so that Dodie could recover from her bout of food poisoning. Dodie had been holed up in the bathroom more or less until they were ready to leave, and Louise was determined to get in there and clean before she had to go and collect Holly. She was already fishing out the bucket and mop as the attentive Lucas helped Dodie out to their car, followed by Mia, carrying the bags. Patrick hung back sullenly in the hall as Louise backed out from the cupboard under the stairs, equipped to clean.

'Oh Christ, what now?'

She joined Patrick at the door to look. Mia had spotted that one of the Shads' front tyres was sagging badly. Lucas, as Dodie drooped in the passenger seat, investigated the boot and announced they had neither pump nor spare. There was talk of the AA. Patrick groaned again, and withdrew to his study, swearing. Louise knew how foolish it would be to follow him in there now and attempt any sort of conversation. Outside, Mia was striding across the drive, watched by Lucas, heading towards the old garage. She seemed to know what she was doing. Louise decided to get on with the bathroom. Perhaps by the time she'd finished, Patrick would be in a more receptive mood.

The bathroom had indeed been left in a dreadful state. After Louise had tackled the toilet and was setting about the pungently splattered pedestal of the washbasin, she heard the sound of the Shads' car finally pulling away. Two down, one to go. But when she went back downstairs, there was no sign of Mia, either. Perhaps she had got a lift from Dodie and Lucas into Newquay? Now was the time, then. No excuses. The sleeping Jamie and the builders apart, it was just her and Patrick.

Patrick didn't like his breakfast early, Louise had come to learn that. He liked to wake his stomach up a bit with tea and fags, so although it was now turned eleven, she put some bacon on on the camping ring Mia had set up in the dining room. She fried an egg to accompany the bacon, made it look nice on the plate, coffee not tea, because he'd be ready to move on to his coffee now, and put it all on a tray for him. Brown sauce, not tomato. He preferred that with a fry-up.

Louise went to the study, knocked and barged the door with the tray.

'Breakfast!' She heard herself but didn't mind. Her nerves had vanished now; she was on a mission. There was the usual smoke to cough against until you got used to it. Mum smiled up at her from that lovely photo, which Louise now dusted regularly when she got a chance at the empty study. She put the tray down on the desk.

'Thought you might fancy it.'

Patrick glanced sidelong at the plate as he swiped the product of a rich, tearing cough into the handkerchief he pulled from his trouser pocket. She couldn't tell if he was still giving her the silent treatment or just exercising his usual morning mood.

'Up to you,' Louise said. 'Anyway, I wanted a word.'

He finished with a sniff. Her pulse frantic, she launched in. She didn't say anything about Kamila, but stuck to her need to keep Holly away from Leeds, and how the house being left to her and Nigel would enable her to do this, without, Louise stressed, affecting Patrick.

'You can't stay here,' he said, when she'd finished. 'I want you out of my house.'

He reached for his packet of cigarettes, his face blank to everything she'd just said.

'It's our house now,' Louise maintained. Beyond them, in the kitchen, a mallet reverberated.

'I'll call the fucking police if I have to.'

Despite the effect of her nerves, Louise realised she wasn't actually frightened of him any more.

'Mum wants me to stay.'

Steadily, she told him about Kamila, about what Mum had passed on to her. If Patrick wouldn't listen properly it was his own lookout; the facts were the facts. On the desk, Mum, in her crown of flowers, averted her eyes, smiling that smile that kept a secret with the side of the picture frame, encouraging her. The top of Louise's head felt light, open, as though all the words she'd kept in there were finally free to spill out. By the time she got to what Mum had told her about the cancer, how Patrick should never have kept it from them and prevented her saying a proper goodbye, Patrick was gasping, hard breaths that made her worry he was having some kind of attack.

'This is complete fucking nonsense!'

'No, it's not.' She felt so calm. There was a far-away crumbling as a wall submitted to the pounding of the mallet.

'You've always been a second-rate person, Louise . . .'

He had to stop. As he gulped a fat tear on to the scarred leather of the desk, Louise was tempted to tell him not to pipe his eye.

'I don't know how many times I have to say this, but I knew nothing about her being ill. The first I knew was when the doctor came, out in the night, after she'd passed out at the supermarket—she was in terrible pain from her stomach. It was the first I knew. They took her into the hospital for tests. Nothing they could do. It was everywhere.'

'But she says—'

'She says nothing!' Patrick spat the words through the fingers caging his face. 'She's dead and gone! There's nothing, you stupid bitch! It all ends in nothing!'

He was looking at her, finally. She was better than him. She'd always been better than him, even when he was somebody. And he was old now.

'Well, you're entitled to your opinion,' she said. 'But I'm telling you, Mum knew she was ill, even if you didn't.'

He barked, half-animal, half-laughter. 'That's more believable,' he said. She was turned to leave. And then, 'You know, she wished you'd never been born.'

It was pathetic. He was pathetic.

'You're a bloody liar, you,' she said. Not said, but shouted at him. For the first time in her life. Leaving, she dared to slam the door.

An hour later, Louise scraped the dead breakfast into the bin and made Jamie a fresh one. He'd just come down. The study was empty; Patrick had gone out, using the front door so he didn't have to brave the chaos of the kitchen, then tramping past on the gravel, taking a route through the back garden. Good riddance, she thought, and got on with feeding Jamie. The sound of that door still made her jump a little after what had happened with Holly. That wouldn't leave her for a long time.

After Jamie had finished eating, she drove them both to the hospital. Holly was dressed, ready to go and excited. Louise should have been ecstatic, but even as she saw Holly's soft beam to Jamie, followed by her complaint to Louise that the jeans she'd brought for her the previous day weren't the right ones, she felt flat. They were forced to wait for the final sign-off from the registrar on duty, whose whereabouts were uncertainly rumoured. Fortunately, Jamie compensated for Louise's slump with his own high spirits, provoking Holly into ever more uncontrolled runs of their excluding laughter.

She wished you'd never been born.

Leaving them to it, Louise went to get herself a cappuccino from the machine outside the ward. As she watched the dismal froth spew erratically against the sides of the thin plastic cup, she recognised the shape of the bleakness that had come with her from the house. It wasn't just the row with Patrick. It was Mum. It was as though a hand holding hers, tight in a deep pocket, the way Louise used to hold Jamie and Hol's hands in her overcoat on the coldest days, big over small, had been withdrawn. She was on her own again. Just like that.

The wait for the registrar stretched on for almost another hour. Then there was a trip to the dispensary for Holly's painkillers and an unnecessary goodbye to her physio, who would be seeing her again in a few days as an outpatient. During all of these duties Louise was itching to get on the phone to Kamila. Surely Kamila could establish contact? It occurred to her that Kamila's untimely trip to the concert was what had disrupted the delicacy of the connection, and that, like faulty broadband, it might be restored.

When they got back from the hospital it was almost five and the builders were already outside, loading up their van. Mia was still nowhere to be seen. Louise, heading straight for the phone in the hall, felt a trill of gut panic as she realised Patrick wasn't back either. He never went for walks, usually. Anything could have happened to him, particularly if he'd taken a whisky bottle out with him, which was more than likely. Louise abandoned her call to Kamila.

'We'd better go and look for him,' she told Jamie. 'I'd never forgive myself if something's happened.'

The fact that Patrick had taken the garden path suggested the cliffs. Louise wondered if Patrick would ever hurt himself. It seemed unlikely, since he'd always been so protective of his health and comfort, but if he'd drunk enough the result may well be the same. He'd enjoy laying it at her door, anyway.

Holly didn't object when Louise settled her in the den with a mug of tea and some snacks. During the journey from the hospital her own ebullience had dwindled, as though the unfamiliar exertion of the drive had worn her out. Louise promised they wouldn't be long, but Holly didn't seem to hear her over the TV. Still, Louise made sure her mobile was safe in her own cardigan pocket. It would be beyond Holly to haul herself as far as the landline in the hall.

It had been raining again, more or less since they'd started out for the hospital, and the ground was in an appalling state. She and Jamie looked for wellies that fitted from the collection in the back porch, but Jamie's feet were too big for any of them, so he had to manage with his trainers. Louise pulled on a muddied green pair that might have belonged to Mum. Stamping her heels down into the chilly rubber, she ached again with the loss of her. She had hoped that her return to the house might reunite them, but there was no change. She had gone, definitely.

Mum had loved Patrick more than anything in the world. Louise should have thought of that, shouldn't she, before she started upsetting him? It was a punishment.

'Come on then, woman.' Jamie held the sagging back door open for her, his exposed sleeve already needled with rain.

It wasn't a day you'd have chosen for a walk. Louise's knees were already protesting on the gradual incline that marked the end of the garden and the overgrown start of the sunken cliff path. As they got to this first summit, Louise could see there were much steeper parts ahead of them, the white line of the path twisting thinly through the high grass like an old scar. There was no sign of Patrick in the view ahead, but there were enough vagaries for blind spots in the lee of the hills where he might be hidden, collapsed or worse. Louise kept looking over the cliff edge, down to the brutal grey rocks below and the frothing mustard sea, fearing to see a liverish scrap of his raincoat, hair fronding in the water. Oh, please God, no, none of them deserved that. She hadn't meant that.

Soon, the steady rain made it hard to see much further ahead than they were walking. The walking itself exhausted Louise, and her slowness made Jamie impatient.

'What about there?' She had toiled to join him at a high point. To their right, the path forked on to a stumpy promontory surmounted by a white, domed building—a lookout, unlikely and municipal in the emptiness, squiggled with graffiti. Louise, who had got a stitch, struggled for the breath to reply. She had never come this far along the clifftops.

'I'll go on ahead,' Jamie said. 'No point you coming, I won't be a sec.'

Louise watched him go, eating up the distance with his loping legs. Before he could reach the lookout point, a figure appeared from the open archway of the dome. Patrick. He descended to meet Jamie as Jamie continued to climb to him, shouting something Louise couldn't hear. Patrick's gait was careful on the muddy, steep decline back to the path, his head bowed by the rain. He was so old now, Louise saw. The weather had whipped his hair so that you could see its underlying sparseness, and even when he reached the flatter ground, and he and Jamie spoke together, there was hesitation in his walk, a failure of vitality. As she watched, Jamie took something from his pocket, followed by something else: a cigarette and a lighter. Patrick bowed to both, eagerly. Jamie didn't follow suit, perhaps because he knew Louise was watching them, but returned both pack and lighter to his pocket. She couldn't have said what she liked less: seeing Jamie with the cigarettes, or that democratic little act of fellowship. None of it was right.

Louise didn't want to share the walk back. She knew that Jamie could have caught her up easily, but he'd have to accommodate Patrick's faltering pace, even slower than hers. She started off without them. The stitch still pinched her side, and she was very wet now, with rain soaking down her neck. She should have been relieved that Patrick was okay, but she felt like shaking him, shaking understanding into him that he couldn't take off like that, all that time when she could have been talking to Kamila in the dry. If Kamila was even able to make contact now. Warm tears mixed with the cold rain on her face as Louise rounded the last cliff to see the back of the house, the surprise of the electric lights inside exposing the unnoticed decline into evening. Probably, it was the same as it had ever been: forced to choose, Mum had chosen him.

'The back door was open,' admonished Mia. She stood in the hall, dry and neat, her damp-shouldered mac draped over the radiator and her shucked boots paired beneath, already stuffed with balled newspaper to keep their shape as they dried, another newspaper sheet spread beneath them to protect the floor. She had made herself one of those teas she liked, with the bag on a string. Louise waited for her to ask where Patrick was, but Mia busied herself with her sludgy teabag, wringing it against the side of the mug with the spoon before fishing it out and cradling it, dripping, to the wastepaper basket under the hall table.

'Patrick decided to go for a walk. Jamie's bringing him back now,' Louise told her. Mia rattled the teaspoon on to a coaster.

'I need to talk to you about something.'

'They'll be back any minute. He's not too steady on his legs these days. Did you go into Newquay?'

Mia turned to Louise. She ignored the yellow tea that steamed by her elbow and tucked her hair back behind each ear, one, two, her eyes on her stockinged feet. Without looking up, she offered Louise a piece of paper.

The lined sheet was torn from a cheap notebook, wrinkled as though it had been smoothed from a ball, its paper yellowed against the young skin of Mia's hand. Mia rotated the page so that the writing was the right way round for Louise to read.

'It was in the boot. I was getting the spare tyre for Lucas, from the old car. I don't know how long it's been in there. Could be years.'

Erratically slanted, the writing was distorted, but its naïve loops were still as familiar as a face: Mum's handwriting. Contact. Thank God. You should always trust in the universe. Louise stared, her relief engulfing understanding. An irritable little hieroglyph in the top left corner of the page refreshed the pen, but even so, the flow of the strokes in bog-standard blue biro broke up on the porous weave of the paper, as though the pen had been running out or the pad had been held upright on a lap to write, so that Mum had had to go back and re-outline some of the letters.

Blind to the words, Louise turned the scrap over, just to be sure. The paper was so thin the pressure from the writing on the other side had indented through, discouraging double usage. That was all there was. She didn't need more. *She wants you to know she loves you.*

Mia shrugged a laugh, but she wasn't amused. 'It's kind of—weird.'

Louise smiled. Was it?

'Don't you think?'

Still smiling, Louise pushed past the marvellous fact of the letters and forced herself to read them.

face any of it. Oh God let it be over. Lies. Every day the same. You get what you deserve. Every day. The way he looks at me, always. Touches even. Hate. Please no more hurting. Hate hate hate hate. The only thing I can do is try to live and

THEY WERE ALL asleep, Nigel most lightly, when his mobile glared and trilled from the chest of drawers in the dim, alien room. The boys didn't wake as he stumbled from bed to retrieve the phone, barking his ankle against an unanticipated coffee table. Sophie muttered and turned.

'You've got to come—'

Patrick had never called him in his life. The precedent brought its own urgency, although Nigel quickly established that it wasn't any kind of medical crisis. He woke Sophie—it was actually only just after midnight—and told her where he was going. She was at the stage of submission to sleep where his departure for the moon would have received the same barely stirring acquiescence. Driving up to the house, Nigel sat for a moment in the car, unwilling to leave its protection, the robust metal and leather mantle of the life he had bought and paid for. God knows what was going on. The car was the only barrier between him and the formless futility that raged around Louise and Patrick, and even Mia now.

Except, incredibly, Mum had left something more. There it was, spalled bricks and biscuit-crumb mortar. A second home. His. Nigel grabbed the car-door handle and stepped back into the world. It had stopped raining, at least.

Sophie had two sisters, one a haematologist and one who called herself a publishing consultant, which meant that she had been an editor before having children and now professed to work part-time. The three women shared holiday villas and took turns to cater vast meals on family anniversaries, visibly the same tetchy, vocal triumvirate chronicled in photographs around their parents' house, posing on ponies or holding trophies, squinting into foreign sunlight in a height order gradually reversed by the passage of time. Although Sophie moaned freely about Olivia's control issues and Ginny's self-entitlement, and holidays inevitably led to tight-lipped conflicts over their children, Nigel never saw either of them without wishing in his heart and soul that these artlessly competent, securely judgemental women were his sisters, too. Instead of which, there was Louise opening the door to him now, all Mystic Meg jewellery and smeared-mascara distress.

'He won't listen to reason.'

Tears, again. It would never be better. If she was determined to stay, then Patrick would have to go, whatever Sophie thought.

Nigel was expecting the study or drawing room, but Louise led him to the den. The air inside was trapped and close. Patrick stood in front of the blank TV screen, smoking, a sheen of sweat on his nose. Mia sat tidily at the edge of the sofa. From the doorway, Nigel felt a paranoid surge of adrenaline, as though they were lying in wait to attack him. Then he saw that Mia was actually relieved by his arrival; Patrick too. He relished the novelty of their absolute attention. He couldn't remember his presence ever affecting Patrick, let alone positively.

'What's all this in aid of?'

This was a phrase that had never left Nigel's mouth before, borrowed from Auntie B and apparently lying in wait for forty years for the occasion.

'You have to tell her to go,' said Patrick.

'I'm not going, I've told him.'

This was Louise. From the sofa, Mia's expression appealed to Nigel.

'This is fucking madness,' said Patrick, madly. Nigel turned. Of the two of them, surely Louise was going to be the more biddable. While irrational, at least she lacked Patrick's volatility. And crucially, she trusted him, her big brother. She believed, after all, in the magic powers of his legal knowledge, as well as all other kinds of magic. He could conjure something out of Mum's will to placate her.

'Read it.' She was holding out a torn piece of notepaper.

The only thing that was obvious was who had written it, although in what extremis Nigel couldn't imagine. *Hate, hate, hate, hate. The way he looks at me always.*

He sat down, close to Mia. 'You've read this?' he asked Patrick.

Patrick shook his head, an infant refusing a detested spoonful. His eyes were closed.

'Why did you hate her?'

Louise's tone was genuinely, wonderingly curious.

'I don't understand,' she said. 'Patrick.'

Patrick's breathing pulled in his chest, painfully. He was overcome by a run of coughs.

'She stopped him writing,' said Mia, unperturbed. 'That's what the Shads said. Maybe that's why she *thought* he hated her, if they'd had a row about it or something.'

'Why would she stop him writing?'

'Maybe she felt jealous about his work,' Mia said. 'She wanted him all to herself.'

'But he was always the jealous one,' said Nigel.

There was not a shred of doubt about that. Say, just as a thought experiment, Nigel himself were to fall uncontrollably in love with someone other than Sophie, in the impossible way of films and novels and memoirs salaciously extracted in newspapers. Mia for example, just to make it as inconvenient as possible. If she were to insist: to be with me you must have no contact with Albie and Olly . . .

Patrick jolted, his voice thinned by coughing, but still vehement. 'You're all talking shit. Bonkers as fucking conkers, the lot of you.'

He faced the three of them.

'I *adored* the woman. Fool for love, fucking idiot. My feelings never changed, never, from the moment I clapped eyes on her.

Jesus—you can't imagine. The world at my feet, well, fuck the world when all you want . . . I tried, Christ, bought the house—thought that would make her happy. Took the thirty pieces of silver. Sold myself down the fucking *river*.'

Patrick rubbed his trembling jaw and looked at Louise. It was a glance of abject directness. Whatever he was about to say, Nigel felt bound to believe him. He had never looked at either of them so democratically, unveiled by hostility or irritation or his magnetic preoccupation with Mum, who was the only person he ever truly wanted to look at. Who could doubt that?

Mia reached to touch Patrick's leg, coaxing him to sit. 'I just thought, with that note, maybe you'd had a row. It makes sense you were pissed off with her if she'd put a stop on your work in some way. I mean, for whatever reason.'

Ignoring her, Patrick stilled the hand rubbing his face on to his opposite shoulder, half cradling himself.

'She didn't stop me doing anything. The thing about Sara . . .' Hopelessly, he hoisted his crooked arm and dropped it, a flightless wing. 'She didn't care enough to stop me doing anything.'

Mia hovered, not touching, still trying to get him to sit. Louise turned away from them and looked to Nigel, an appeal immediately at the ready.

'You know they're getting married,' Nigel told her, with some satisfaction. *Enough*.

At this Patrick growled, craning back to him. Nigel flinched, but all he was aiming for was the note, which he swiped from his hand. Louise, Nigel could see, was too shocked by what she had just heard to register the capitulation. For seconds Patrick parsed the scrap of paper, head craned back and arm fully stretched.

> *—face any of it. Oh God let it be over. Lies. Every day the same. You get what you deserve. Every day.*

The way he looks at me, always. Touches even. Hate. Please no more hurting. Hate hate hate hate. The only thing I can do is try to live and—

'You can't be.' Louise faced Mia. 'She would have told me. Mum—Kamila would have known.' This, to Patrick, who paid no attention.

When he spoke, his voice was robustly irritable: old, of course, but entirely unbroken.

'"*The way he looks at me, always.*" How do you think I fucking looked at her? It didn't change from the moment I saw her, out in the arse end of nowhere. Love. I looked at her with love. That was the way I looked at her. And she loathed it.'

Patrick shook the flimsy sheet, offering it to whoever wanted to claim it. 'Not at the beginning. But hate—fuck me.'

He smiled down, at a reality that still amazed him.

'Hate hate hate. That was your mother's department.'

Then

1997

LOUISE WANTED her mum. She was over six months pregnant, beginning to get huge, and for the first time in the three years they'd been together, Warren had completely forgotten her birthday. When he didn't turn up for his tea she had a surge of hope that he was out doing last-minute shopping, but he had just gone straight to the pub from work. He came in late, his eyes pink from smoking dope in the van with the lads, grumbling there was nothing in the fridge as he ate an indiscriminate assortment of the food that was actually in there. Then, stoned and beery, he took her into the bedroom and shagged her. As Louise rocked against the weight of him (they had to do it from the side, she'd got so big already), she stared at the Artex on the top half of the wall in front of her, which was coming off in patches like a disease, and was overwhelmed by the shittiness of their flat, of Warren's unromantic demands, of their life to come with the baby and no money. She wanted her mum. She wanted her so badly it was like the worst sort of craving, like no way she'd ever wanted her before, as though she had that thing that supposedly made you eat coal but in her case it was wanting to see her mum. As Warren came, Louise reached out to replace a triangle of wallpaper beneath the Artex that drooped from its seam. She hadn't chosen it. She hadn't chosen bloody anything.

After Warren left for work next morning, Louise used her so-called housekeeping to buy a ticket on a coach to Cornwall, a journey that was no joke with a pregnant bladder. She didn't leave Warren a note, or call him on the mobile he'd recently acquired. Louise didn't care. It was like she was in a dream and the only way she could wake up was by talking to her mum. Which was strange, because Mum had never been much of a talker.

She arrived in Newquay in the glare and traffic of teatime in the summer season, and used the last of her money getting a taxi out to the house. Why had she never thought of this before? It was well over ten years since the last disastrous trip Mum and Patrick had taken up to see her, when Patrick had ranted about her teenage foray into meditation. There had never been another meeting, let alone the promised family Christmas. Various plans had been postponed, one by one, then lapsed into cancellations, until the lack of contact established itself as a habit. Still, Louise's intense teenage familiarity with the few pictures Mum had sent of the house when she and Patrick first moved in were enough to produce a lurch of recognition as they approached the drive, followed by the lurch of difference in seeing the house as it was, unframed and real. Heart speeding, she paid the taxi and pressed the ivory teat of the doorbell in its tarnished brass dome. She didn't hear the bell ring inside, and endured an uncertain interlude wondering if it was broken, and if not, whether it would be rude persistence to ring again. Finally, by a combination of vain ringing and timid knocking, she brought Patrick to the door.

Patrick himself was unchanged, except for a new wildness to his eyebrows that added to his ferocity. He didn't recognise her, of course. Even when she said 'Louise', it didn't register immediately.

When she said she'd come to see her mother, his face altered to a more pointed unfriendliness.

'It's you, is it?' He took her in differently, noting her mounded belly. 'Christ.' Although Louise had been nothing but excited about the baby from its first moment, one sweep of Patrick's eyes found the scabby Artex and Warren's indifference.

'She's not here. She's gone out.'

Louise's suspicion that Patrick was lying didn't form immediately. It took the minutes she waited on the doorstep, lowering herself on to the worn grey stone to relieve her swollen ankles and pulsing feet while Patrick called a cab to take her back to the bus station, until his failure to invite her inside suggested a motive other than his traditional hostility. What if her mum was a couple of walls away, ignorant of her arrival? What could Louise do to announce her presence without provoking Patrick? Sluggishly, she rallied herself.

'Could I just see her for a minute, do you think? I'll go straight back.'

Patrick put down the phone. 'She isn't here, I told you. She's gone up to London.'

It wasn't as though he was scared of offending her. The call finished, he told her the cab would arrive in about fifteen minutes and left her, the open front door his only gesture towards hospitality. Sitting on the step, Louise imagined her mother at the upstairs window, forlornly watching her departure, like an advert that had intrigued her as a child when it appeared in Auntie B's magazines—'Things happen after a Badedas bath'. You saw the bare back of a woman, a draped silken sheet just short of revealing the crack of her gently rounded arse, while she looked out of a window at a handsome knight on horseback in the courtyard below her. Louise had been too young to understand the caption's implication about what was really supposed to happen after the bath; to her, the scene always appeared to be one of mournful farewell, not anticipation, the woman held captive and unable to be with her departing knight.

Mum had made a promise to Patrick. She could never, ever break it. It was an enchantment.

There was no sound from the corridor where Patrick had disappeared (the one that in fact led to his study). The rest of the house was quiet. Moving as softly as she could, Louise edged into the hall, the smell of damp rebuffing her. She had to try. Excruciated, she placed her foot on the bottom stair, releasing a steady creak from the warped wood. After a second or two, with no reaction from Patrick, she braved the next step. By the fifth, it became clear that he could hear nothing from wherever he was and she picked up the pace, still muffling her steps by keeping her heels suspended. Reaching the top landing, a desperate relief overtook her and she ran through the first door she saw, which led to the empty bathroom. The room opposite was their bedroom. That was empty too. The silence told her that Patrick hadn't been lying. Mum wasn't hiding anywhere, but nor was she waiting.

When the cab arrived, Louise poked her head back into the echoing hall and called, 'That's me off, then.' Patrick bellowed a dismissive goodbye from the direction of his study. Louise had to wait hours at the station for the coach to take her back to Leeds, but it wasn't until she was safely in her seat that she sobbed her disappointment into the bristled fag-stink of her moquette headrest.

NIGEL HAD TAKEN a day from his holiday allowance to help Cally move out of their flat. In fact, she had already arranged for her father to help, so his gesture was redundant, as well as, according to her, both pathetic and typical. The final word she produced was *abject*, her satisfaction in alighting on it obscuring even her irritation. Since their mutual affection had evaporated, Cally's predominant emotion towards him was exposed, jaggedly and angrily, as contempt. Time was, Cally had said things like 'You're so *abject*' and Nigel had nodded, hangdog and obliging, and she had gathered him in and kissed the top of his head, perhaps fingering his ten-pence-sized bald spot fondly as she did so. No more. In the terrible weeks since she had confessed to sleeping with her pupil master, the end of that not-quite affair, and her determination to break up with Nigel despite his immediate willingness to forgive her for it, Cally had become increasingly furious. Nigel knew that he wasn't the bad guy, but he couldn't return her fury, even as she escalated into behaving like a soap opera bitch. He didn't want her to leave, but he longed for it all to be over. An eczematous rash had crept from the crooks of his elbows down his forearms, reaching the interstices of his fingers, where it itched ragingly, despite the assiduous film of hydrocortisone cream he applied morning and night. Seeing him screw the midget cap carefully back on the tube of cream one recent evening had been enough to send Cally roaring from the bathroom.

Having put in formally for a day off, Nigel was loath to withdraw in case explanations for the withdrawal were required. It was bad enough that the news of his girlfriend leaving him was being metabolised through the firm. He had been sleeping on the sofa for some time, to Cally's further annoyance (although she didn't want to share a bed with him and hadn't offered to take the sofa herself), which meant that he slept badly, assailed by traffic noise, the street light that shone through the slats of the living-room blind, and the goblin light of the VCR if he forgot, as he usually did, to lean a cushion against it at bedtime. Even so, as dawn broke on the morning Cally was due to go, it was the noise from the bedroom that brought Nigel to consciousness, as she opened and shut drawers for the last time. It was really going to happen. She was leaving him.

Thank God they hadn't bought a place together. It had been during the discussions Nigel had persistently initiated about them entering the housing market that Cally had announced her infidelity. Since there was no way he could cover the rent on his own and it was a one-bedroom flat, he would soon be moving himself. Nigel didn't feel sentimental about this, leaving these expanses of MDF in the charmless end of Hammersmith. All his sentimentality was reserved, still, for Cally. Thinking about her going made his fingers itch. He doubted he would ever manage to find anyone else of her calibre to be his girlfriend.

While Cally tracked between bedroom and bathroom, swerving past boxes and adding to others, Nigel dressed and ate a meek bowl of cereal, trying to keep his spoon quiet. It would be best, and most dignified, if he got out before Cally's father arrived. There was a library a few streets away, and a cybercafé even closer, if he wanted to check his work email. Carefully, he fitted the heavy laptop that was his pride and joy into its dedicated backpack. It was time.

The bedroom looked stripped and utilitarian without the ropes of beads and mismatched earrings and medley of tubes and pots on the dresser, Cally's stacks of paperbacks by the bed. She had removed the duvet cover, but not the duvet. The walls were bare; he didn't own anything in a frame. Nigel noted that Cally was zipping an engorged cylindrical sports bag that technically belonged to him. He decided to let it go.

'So . . .'

She glared at him.

'I'm off. Leave you to it,' he said.

Just as he leaned in, muttering, 'All the best,' her expression softened and she gave him a fierce, proper hug. She even patted the top of his head.

'Let me know about the phone bill. You've got the address.'

He said he had. She was going to stay with her parents in Blackheath for a while. She said she would be gone by lunchtime, all being well. And that was that. Just for a moment, Nigel could have wept, but didn't. He struck out for the cybercafé, which was more congenial than he had feared. Sitting among the foreign students, he drank serial weak cappuccinos and got a surprising amount of work done. At lunchtime, he went to another café and lingered over his chicken baguette. Even so, when Nigel loitered back into the top of their road just after two, the small hire van was still parked outside the flat, its back open to reveal its trove of boxes and bags. As Nigel hesitated, the main door to the block opened and Cally's dad backed out, balancing a box stacked with pans against his modest paunch. Cally followed, arm splayed to stop the door swinging back on her, talking back at someone inside the hallway. She kept her arm spread to hold the door for them, her posture helpful, either patronising or polite; it was impossible to read without seeing the other person.

It was his mother.

She walked from the building, a little tentative, chatting to Cally. The two of them had never met. Since Sara never visited, Nigel had never invited her. The last time he had seen her was just after he'd qualified almost six years before, when he and Cally were supposed to be travelling to St Ives, but Cally had had to cry off with what turned out to be glandular fever. Since then there had been only the usual cards: birthday and Christmas. Nigel advanced, bewildered.

'There you are.' His mother said this with such immediate, low-key exasperation that he wondered if a letter or phone message had gone astray.

It must have been obvious to her that Cally was moving out, if they hadn't actually had a conversation about it inside, but Sara said goodbye to Cally in the same unembellished way as she had addressed him. He and Cally reiterated their own embarrassed goodbye, punctuated by an even more embarrassed handshake with Cally's dad, Adam, and redundant introductions between the two parents. Cally handed Nigel the keys they had arranged for her to post through the letterbox. Distracted by Sara, there was no opportunity to watch the van depart elegiacally out of their road. When he suggested they go out, Mum said it would be too much bother and couldn't they have a cup of tea upstairs?

Nigel had kept the kettle, although when he opened the cupboard door above it, the row of mugs was gapped like a badly kept mouth. Aware of Mum's gaze, he patted his hair down over his bald spot as she watched him make the tea. She herself looked the same: sharp-eyed, idiosyncratically glamorous, her hair more grey than gold now, but still a statement. A statement along the lines of *I'm not like other people, so don't assume anything about me.*

One of them would have to speak.

'How's Patrick?'

'Fine. The same. Fine.'

He put the tea down in front of her. It was always a bit of a surprise that she didn't smoke. It would have suited her.

'Lucky you were in.'

She was always more northern than he remembered as well. When she got hold of the handle of her mug, Nigel was shocked to see her hands tremble, so much that a drop of tea slopped on to the tabletop. He ignored the lapse, seeing that she wouldn't acknowledge it herself. Was she nervous, then?

'So. To what do I owe . . .'

'There's an exhibition I wanted to see. Patrick wasn't keen.'

He was about to ask her about the exhibition—he had never known her to be interested in art—but she interrupted him.

'Cally. What's that short for then?'

'Calliope.'

Mum snorted a laugh and gulped at her tea. Typical, it meant. Typical Nigel. Just the sort of girlfriend you would have. Ex-girlfriend. She saw him watching her fingers, to see if their tremor had stopped. She put the mug down on the table and placed her hand out of sight on her lap.

'Ah well. Plenty more fish in the sea.'

Nigel disallowed the blood rush that followed this dead offering, the urge to toss hot tea in his mother's face. What the fuck do you know? What the fuck do you care? But something of his rage must have conveyed itself to her—a shift in facial colour, the aversion of his eyes. She hitched her chair back from the table, and seemed to think better of whatever she was about to say next.

The creases between his fingers itched horribly. What in the name of God did she want, he wondered. She was definitely here for a reason. That was the thing about Mum: she didn't do anything without a reason. Or rather, if there wasn't a reason—an advantage, let's face it—you wouldn't catch her doing it. When he met her eye, Mum looked away, feigning interest in the view over the asphalt forecourt of the Territorial Army building next door. In her lap, her forefinger worried at some loose skin around her thumbnail. Her bag was at her feet, a waxed Liberty shopper with tape round the handle that betrayed nothing about the nature of her errand.

'Do you remember when I left—before I left, I mean? When I met Paddy?'

'Of course.'

'Yes, you weren't that little.'

She continued to watch the deserted building. Her tone was remote, but relaxed.

'But you remember, when we talked about it, and I asked you for advice. You were always so sensible.'

Her gaze shifted to him; acute, unchangingly blue. No one had eyes like hers.

'You remember. I asked you what I should do.'

He did. He remembered too much. With the nostalgia of walking into a smell, Nigel reinhabited his childhood desire to protect her.

'I let you decide,' she said.

'Yes.'

It was all he could bring himself to say. As ever, he was a disappointment to her. Her sigh extended into draining the last of the tea and slamming the mug on the table surface. She managed to make the gesture look dashing, a little dangerous. A buccaneer, unlike her son.

'Well. You make your own bed, and you lie in it.'

Already, Mum was getting to her feet. Nigel scrabbled his fingers against each other for a convulsive few seconds. It was clear that he'd have to do the asking.

'Do you need somewhere—do you want to stay the night?'

Oh no, she said, and explained that she was staying with her friends the Shads, who lived in Kew.

'Just a pair of knickers and a toothbrush,' she told him, indicating the shopper.

He wasn't sure he believed that, when he thought about it that night, a sour bottle of Bulgarian corner-shop red to the bad. He wished he'd pushed her about the exhibition as well. What exactly were you going to see, Mum? What did you think about it? What did it, in fact, make you feel?

Downstairs, she paused with one foot on the front step.

Have you heard anything from Louise lately?'

Of course not. They had pared down their communication even beyond Mum's, purely to Christmas, and even those cards unreliably on his part.

'She's having a baby.'

'Oh.' What else was there to say?

'Poor bitch.'

Apart from that. When he kissed his mother goodbye, one kiss on each cheek, the way he did now automatically, she started at the contact of the second, her face already withdrawn. But he could see the gesture had made her smile at his affectation. He waved her off, all the way out of sight, even when it was clear she wasn't going to turn back to see him. A straight figure with her bizarre cloud of hair, the bag she was carrying almost weightless. Once she had gone, Nigel turned back to the empty stairs, raking the raw joints of his fingers. Thank God for hydrocortisone.

Now

WAKING TO the sound of the electrician's van, Mia's spirit lifted: he had really turned up, and in a few hours there would be nothing left to thwart her leaving. Of course it hadn't mattered to anyone except her that without her supervision, Andy and his men wouldn't be paid and the kitchen would languish unfinished, but her sense of order had imposed its own timetable. Mia had resolved not to leave until the kitchen was done, and Mary Poppins-like, she had prevailed. During what Andy had almost promised would be his crew's last week, she still hoped that one of the email applications she had scattered into the ether might seed itself into a job opportunity. As that week had run fruitlessly into the following, with electric wires still hanging bare from the holes drilled for spots, and her inbox barren, Mia rang her mother to tell her that she'd be coming home for a while, for a break. She packed, then repacked. There wasn't much to take. The electrician was elusive, working on other jobs.

In the meantime, Patrick pressed harder each day for them to get married. To placate him, Mia made the call to the registrar. The date they agreed on was securely weeks ahead; its prospect calmed Patrick down. Mia knew that by the time it came she'd be long gone.

Patrick thought he was giving her something, and for months she'd believed it was all she was ever likely to get. What he had actually given her was a ring that had belonged to his own mother, apparently never worn by Sara (Mia had enquired, suspiciously). It was pretty, art nouveau diamond chips and garnet, too uncontemporary for her to choose herself but clearly quite valuable, and it was easy enough to wear it on her engagement finger, if only to make a statement to Louise.

Showing Louise that note of her mother's had seemed like such a good idea, a subtle detonation to create a fault line along the aggravating supremacy of Sara and Patrick, clearing a space for their marriage. Admittedly, she too, misdirected by Dodie, had failed to understand the hatred expressed in that desperate fragment. She had accommodated it as evidence that Patrick's first marriage hadn't been such a fairy tale that it wouldn't permit a second. Well, she had been right about that, just not about anything else. And now there were consequences.

'Don't be in any doubt, I kept my side of the bargain. Did everything she asked me to, this house, *Bloody Empire*, everything . . . Jesus. Every day. Bloody fool I was. Madness.'

Louise, though, still refused to believe that her mother had felt anything for Patrick except devotion. She was supported in this by the woman at the end of the phone, her sensitive, as she called her. And now, whipped into a sort of frantic affront by their engagement, not only was she refusing to leave, but she had told Mia that if she married Patrick, she would make sure they were both chucked out of the house. Nigel kept tempering this, but Mia had really had enough. Of all of them, Sara most definitely included. Even if they stayed, the house would never properly be theirs. With property no longer clouding her thoughts, Mia wondered if she could have been having some very specific, low-key kind of breakdown, possibly connected to Jonathon and the MA. If she had believed in that kind of thing, she might even have said that something had possessed her.

Patrick's cough was worse and since Mia couldn't be bothered to rouse him, he spent almost the entire day in bed, coming downstairs only when called for supper. After so many days of apocalyptic rain, another bout of freakishly hot weather had descended. The unnaturally close feel inside the house was enhanced by the presence of Jamie and Holly, who drooped around, indolent and bored, sleeping almost as late as Patrick and, like him, nocturnally active. The school-holiday vibe enhanced Mia's own inert mixture of longing and apprehension over her postponed future. While Patrick slept, she sunbathed in the garden like a teenager. Only the rare chill that sliced into you as soon as the sun went behind a cloud reminded you it was April.

Now that the builders had dwindled to the sole, erratically appearing electrician, Holly's excursion to physiotherapy was the spine of the day. As usual, Nigel and Sophie chose this time that Louise was out with Holly to come round from their hotel. The children were keen to wake Jamie, who was affably prepared to kick a ball around with them once he was up. While Nigel fielded their enthusiasm, Sophie disappeared to tackle the unprocessed rooms upstairs. When she first declared this project, Mia had deployed the ring that Patrick had given her to ensure that nothing was thrown away without her agreement. But then Sophie unearthed a signed rehearsal copy of a Pinter play that Mia herself would have stuffed straight into a bin liner, and she had relaxed her unauthorised vigilance.

Nigel let the little boys run round the garden, with an eye to the cliffs, as Mia applied facial sunscreen, just to be on the safe side. Nigel, pacing, watched her. It was probably her last opportunity, she realised, to interrogate him about the note and its aftermath. The box was well and truly open. Better to tidy that up, too, before she left.

'Dodie definitely said Sara stopped Patrick writing. She said Lucas couldn't forgive her for it,' she said. He didn't seem at all surprised by her raising the subject. Pleased, rather.

'From what I know, he never seems to stop,' Nigel said. 'Being successful at it—that's another matter. You can hardly blame Mum for that.'

Mia squinted up at him, framed against the sun.

'Patrick says they all stopped putting his stuff on because they didn't like his politics. You know, after *Bloody Empire*. That's what he said when I first came here to ask him about his writing.'

'Ah yes, the establishment conspiracy.'

Nigel planted his feet, arms crossed, savouring what he was about to say.

'It is possible, you know, his plays just weren't any good,' he said. 'Have you read them? The people Patrick badmouths weren't exactly shying away from lefties in the eighties, were they? I mean, Thatcher wasn't running the National Theatre, as far as I know. Maybe he was writing rubbish, or maybe he just pissed too many people off. I couldn't tell you. It's all nonsense to me, to be frank.' He lifted his shoulders, exhorting himself further than she had ever seen him dare. 'I mean, the theatre. Come on. All that bloody *shouting*.'

Immediately worried by his own vehemence, he shuffled his feet closer and looked down. Mia quite liked him, really. There was a lot they agreed on.

'What did your mum think of them, though?' she asked. 'His plays?'

'I'm not sure she saw any of them, apart from *Bloody Empire*.

You know, the famous one. I don't have a clue what she thought of it. Anyway—it bought her this.' Nigel waved back at the house.

That was weird, wasn't it, that something you made up out of your head, and not even something useful, like an iPad, could turn into a building? Mia considered saying this to Nigel. He would have got it.

'Weird, though. It was her name in the play, wasn't it?' She felt quite proud of herself for remembering; she'd only read it the once.

'And there any similarity ends.'

'So it wasn't, like, based on her?'

Nigel stared. 'You mean, was my mother raped by a gang of squaddies? Certainly not! Surely you haven't mistaken Patrick for a *realist*?'

There was a squawk from the boys. They had spotted Jamie, rubbing his densely decorated forearms across his pale, bare chest as he slouched into the garden from the back door. Olly punted the football powerlessly towards him.

'Give us a minute!'

Booting the ball back to Olly, Jamie dropped to the grass, rooting for his cigarette packet in the jeans he wore slung below his pubic bone. Nigel immediately started after the boys and tried to divert them from the sight of their idol smoking. Jamie lit and inhaled, staring down at the grass and knuckling the back of his bedhead as he blew out the first deep catch of smoke. His hair, like Albie's, was curly, a shared link back to Sara, according to Nigel. He actually wasn't bad-looking underneath all the dodgy decisions. Although Mia had become familiar with his fidgety unease, today it seemed to have cranked up a notch. While he smoked he piked his knees up and stretched them back out, rested back on his elbows and then quickly changed his mind, sitting up again before resuming his previous position. Mia kept her face to the sun, waiting.

'There's summat . . .'

It would probably be about the army again. She didn't blame him for not breaking the news to Louise. If he was smart he'd just do a bunk, like she was planning to. Mia had decided she would go at night, a proper vanishing. *Never complain, never explain, babe.*

Next to her, Jamie, pained, pulled his phone from the front pocket of his jeans, thumbed across the screen.

'What d'you reckon?'

Mia reared away from the image he held out to her: flesh, nipples, thong.

'I can't believe it, me.'

His own face was averted. It wasn't a joke, then, or a come-on. He wanted a reaction, but not that. Mia looked again, properly. It was amateur, not porn, a phone shot with flare at the top, no face, hairs and imperfections.

'She must have nicked it out of me pocket when I was asleep.'

Holly. Mia took the phone from him, forced a proper look. Despite her still limited capacity to move, Holly had apparently trekked to filch Jamie's phone during the night, posed somewhere—possibly the bathroom, since it was the only room with a lock—and sent the shots (there was more than one, but Mia declined further revelation) to an unidentified number.

'It must be this bloke,' said Jamie. 'Fucking pervert. Jesus. She's not been fourteen five minutes.'

Apparently Louise had warned him to keep Holly away from phones. It was unlikely she thought this might be what Holly was up to. Mia wondered why the girl hadn't had the wit to delete the messages from the sent folder. Perhaps she had been interrupted?

'She's mad on him,' said Jamie. 'I mean, proper. I can't tell Mum, she'll go mental.'

Then he glanced at her. 'Even more mental.'

Leaving the phone on the grass between them, he unfolded himself to his feet and mooched after the ball Albie had toddled into a ragged flowerbed nearby. The boys rampaged as he looped the ball effortlessly, high in the air above them. Mia looked down at the phone's dark sheen. For the first time she thought that Louise's attempts to protect Holly might not be completely deranged. But if someone wanted something so badly, how could you stop them?

Earlier that morning, as Holly and Louise were about to set off for physio, Louise had disappeared back into the house for her keys while Mia was struggling to wheel the emptied dustbin back from the end of the drive. As Mia passed, she had acknowledged Holly, sitting in the front seat of the rusted Nissan with the door open to circulate some air. She was perched with her legs stretched out on to the gravel—bending them still presented her with problems, and even with the seat cranked back as far as it would go, getting into the car made her grimace. Seeing Mia's glance at the car's beaten-out fender, Holly had launched into a meandering account of how many times Louise's car had been broken into, because the thinness of the doors made it possible to bend them back easily and jack the lock.

'Piece of shit,' she remarked unaggressively. And then: 'My boyfriend's car's really lush?'

It was a BMW, apparently. Holly sighed. 'We just drive around, it's just, yeah . . . talking and that, in his car. We just talk and talk, for like hours sometimes. I tell him everything.'

The bin's right wheel was hinking on the stones, making it hard for Mia to manoeuvre. Her grunt of effort as she tried to push was mistaken by Holly as conversational, encouraging her to continue.

'He knows everything about me? It's the best. He's like, such a good listener? No one never listens to me, 'cos I talk all the time. Our Jamie says I talk a load of shit.'

'Right.'

Mia kicked gravel from under the wheel to clear the way.

'One time, it was raining so hard? I was just like soaked and Nish picked me up and said I'm not taking you home till you're dry and he give me his T-shirt and turned all the heaters up and we just drove round, I don't even know where, and he stopped and got me a hot chocolate and he listened to all like about me mum and home and me dad going and how shit school stuff is and that.'

Mia attempted to steer the bin, as Holly watched, her feelings elsewhere.

'It was the best. I mean, it's all that matters, isn't it? Love. He loves me.'

The wheel had finally released and Mia trundled the bin back up to its place, oddly encumbered by a sense of Holly's claim to superiority over her. The shots on the phone now made sense of this, as well as her unusual friendliness. *He loves me.* Maybe he did treat her well, and the age gap was an unfortunate barrier to a rare affinity. Or more likely he'd been grooming her—hot chocolate and special cuddles—and Jamie was right that the police should be called. But whatever they did, the girl who had sent those photos was never again going to be happy just with *Homes Under the Hammer* and a trip to the shopping centre with her girlfriends. Louise was fighting a losing battle. It hadn't taken much: a flash car and a bit of attention.

Mia's left thumb spun the engagement ring on her finger. It needed adjusting to fit her properly.

'Miss?'

The call came from behind her, inside the house. It was the electrician, a small guy around her own age whose air of tetchy contempt was seemingly contained only by his limited English.

He lifted his toolbox to indicate that he was ready to go. Mia followed him into the kitchen. There it was, finished—perhaps the brushed steel had been a mistake after all—a tidy mound of dust waiting in the middle of the floor to be bagged, an offcut of flex and a spare switchboard on the immaculate counter. Putting down his toolbox, the electrician stood at the door and snapped the lights on, one by one, brusquely swivelled the dials of the dimmers to demonstrate the work he had done. Mia hadn't bothered to find out which country he actually came from.

'Okay?'

Mia agreed that it was. It was finished, everything worked. She had kept her promise and now she was free. With a departing glance at her arse, he left her to stand there, contemplating the transformation. *He loves me, that's all that matters.* Muted squeals came from outside as the little boys kicked the ball back to the big boy. The way the light from the spots fell, you could be anywhere. *Never complain, never explain.* It wasn't nothing, what she'd done.

THE FORCE OF the rain was astonishing after the days of unusual heat. Even so, Louise was the only person in the house to be woken by it, so when she opened the door to Nigel, she felt glad of the company. She never liked to be quiet in the mornings.

'Nidge.'

Louise took the huge, clown-striped golf umbrella he had started to shake on to the mat and led him to the kitchen, where it could drip in the new sink.

'Very smart,' he said, looking round. Louise had to concede that it was. Since Kamila had conveyed Mum's approval of the changes, she felt much better about Mia's presumption. Nigel sat in one of the old chairs they'd moved back in with the pine table, which now looked even shabbier amid the new fittings. He asked some formulaic questions about Holly's recovery, but she could tell that his interest was elsewhere. He and the family were travelling home later that day. Louise braced herself to talk about money, as they had agreed.

'I've been thinking,' she told him. 'You might be right.'

It was all different since she'd known about Patrick, about his true feelings. How could she think of continuing to live here with him and Mia? Even Mum's own view had undergone a change in the last days. If anything, she thought Louise (and Nigel) should take the house outright and Patrick be damned, but Nigel had persuaded Louise that this would be legally difficult, if not impossible. Kamila had been a godsend, as ever. As she had pointed out, the main thing was that Holly was improving every day.

Sitting across the table from Nigel, Louise set it out to him, making sure that they agreed. He would give her her half of the money the house was worth, and with that she'd buy a place for herself and the kids, far away from all the trouble that waited in Leeds. She could see that Nigel hadn't been expecting this at all.

'Right,' he said. 'Great. I'll . . . crack on, if you're sure.'

He told her that she should have a solicitor to handle her side of their agreement, which had to be drawn up formally. Surely that was money for old rope, she pointed out, with his qualifications. It wasn't as though she didn't trust him.

Nigel ran his hand down his face. His skin was pink, dewed with raindrops, or perhaps sweat. It was still clammily warm, despite the wet.

'Weezer.'

He still remembered, then. Perhaps he even remembered it better than she did, the time before Patrick, although he never talked about it. That day, when Dad had called them in to tell them Mum had gone, Nigel standing next to her, the trapped summer air in the small, dark living room of their terrace, the garish pattern of the carpet. The unprecedented formality of being summoned by their dad in this way had inculcated them both with dread before he'd even opened his mouth. Louise's memory didn't include any of his actual words, just the import of them soaking into her as she stared down at the uneven way the inside legs of her bibbed tomato-red shorts rode up into her granular white thighs. She had cried. Nigel hadn't, and had got credit for it. Nothing had been the same again.

Much later, when everything had been rearranged because Dad couldn't be expected to work and look after children, Auntie B had put up a picture of Nigel on the china cabinet, to replace the actual Nidge who had gone away to school. When Louise saw him again, it was impossible to imagine them playing trampolines on the bed. 'Give your brother a cuddle, then,' Auntie B had urged, and Louise had hugged this tall new boy with long hair and odd clothes who didn't talk much like Nidge any more or even smell like him; that warm, stale, boy-smell of body and earth and chocolate biscuits. He hadn't hugged her back. She could feel how embarrassed he was by her, and he had stayed embarrassed ever since.

She put her hand out, across the table.

'Don't look so worried,' she said. 'You've got to trust in the universe. Things have a way of working out.'

Nigel didn't respond, but for once he kept his hand there, beneath hers. She could feel him gathering all his breath. 'You know what she did,' he said, finally. 'Mum—'

There was a wail from upstairs—an animal howl. Nigel was faster than her on the stairs, with her knees. When Louise reached the bedroom, Nigel was already sitting next to Patrick on the bed, patting his back, murmuring. No blood, no disaster.

Mia had gone. At first Louise thought it was just Patrick panicking because Mia had got up early and gone out without telling him, which he never liked, but as he insisted, she saw that it was true: the room had been stripped back to what belonged there. There was nothing left in Mia's side of the wardrobe, nothing in her allocated drawers. The zipped bags of toiletries were gone from the bathroom, and downstairs, her jackets and coat had been removed from their hooks, her aligned pairs of shoes taken from the mat. The dining room table was bare of the laptop she kept on it, always exactly parallel to the edge. She'd buggered off, all right. Like a thief in the night.

Patrick was wild, demanding they call the police. Nigel assured him that there was nothing the police could do. Mia was free to go. She hadn't taken anything that wasn't hers, had she?

'I'll call them myself.' Patrick struggled up. They let him go.

'Bloody hell,' said Nigel, still on the bed. 'What's she playing at?'

He looked upset himself. Louise felt excited; more than that—relieved. Mia had seen sense, pure and simple. Mum was at work, somewhere.

'It wouldn't have been right, them getting married. A young girl like that.'

Holly stood at the door. 'What's happened?'

While bleared, she was already made up and dressed, quite carefully, even her hair straightened, so the noise couldn't have woken her up. Louise thought of Holly's Valium from the hospital, and wondered if they should give Patrick one to calm him down. She could hear him shouting on the phone.

'She must have left a note or something,' said Nigel. But Mia hadn't. Not in the bedroom, not downstairs. There were no voicemail messages on either of their phones. When the police rang back to see if everything was okay, following Patrick's garbled rant to 999, they were advised not to waste any more police time. Between them, she and Nigel realised that they didn't know Mia's surname, let alone any details of her family, although, as Nigel pointed out, there was enough paperwork around the place to repair this ignorance and allow pursuit of her if it was really needed. Was it, though?

Louise went to retrieve the Valium packet from Holly's room. She hadn't seen Patrick so agitated since she was a teenager, and seldom so mobile. She'd expected him to take to the study with a whisky bottle, but instead he kept ranging around downstairs from room to room, talking, talking, talking. Most of it swearing, of course, tirades about faithlessness and futility and the folly of age. Nigel shadowed him tentatively all the while, like a netball marker without the confidence to try for the ball. At least Patrick didn't seem likely to make a break out of the house this time. Amid all this, Holly started trying to persuade Louise that she should go out to do a food shop, as she'd planned, but Louise was determined to stick around until she could see Patrick felt a little calmer.

He was coughing unstoppably, doubled over, and he wasn't a good colour. All this might kill him. She knew he wouldn't take a Valium if she suggested it, and possibly not even if Nigel did, and decided on grinding a tablet into a heavily sweetened cup of tea. As she went down to the kitchen, Holly planted herself at the bottom of the stairs.

'Leave him, Mum, he'll be fine.'

'I'm sure he will, but I'm not taking any chances.'

'Just—go shopping. If you miss the shops you'll be kicking yourself. There's nothing in.'

'There's plenty in.'

God knows why she had such a bee in her bonnet about the shopping, but she'd been like that since the accident; you could never tell what would set her off. Normally, Louise was indulgent, but there was too much going on. She snapped at Holly that they could go to Tesco on the way back from physio tomorrow: she would have to sit in the car park and lump it. It was a tone Louise hadn't taken with her in a long time. Used to the protection of being an invalid, Holly recoiled. She was gathering herself to argue when the doorbell shrilled uncertainly, its circuit loose.

'I'll get it!' Holly headed across the hall with reckless speed, careless of her crutches. Louise called after her to be careful. Patrick was already in the hall, at the midpoint of his pacing route, with Nigel close at hand. Nigel moved to open the door. Glimpsing black hair, Louise expected Mia, and she could see by the tilt of Patrick's head that he too was hopeful. But it was a young man the hair belonged to; as he spoke, she could see a sliver of him, black-haired and brown-skinned from the angle she had. There was a polite mumble, and Nigel swung the door open to let him in.

The man hovered, reluctant. He was small, Louise could see, and his posture was wired as though in anticipation of a fight, his eyeline darting back to the showy car, now visible, parked behind him in the drive.

'You're all right. Is Holly about?' The man still spoke quietly, with a strong Leeds accent. That's when she knew. *Him*.

Holly swung up to the doorway and clipped Nigel on the back of the calf with one of her crutches, so that he took an automatic step back. 'Get out of the way!'

'All right, mate—she wants to talk to me.' The man's tone remained soft, wheedlingly reasonable.

Louise's attempt to cry out was stifled by shock.

'I'm afraid that won't be possible. I suggest you go before I call the police.' Thank God, Nigel had twigged. She was glad that he had a good few inches and about a stone over that piece of shit.

'What the hell's going on?' Patrick looked as paralysed as Louise.

'You can't stop me talking to him! He hasn't done nothing!'

'You her dad?'

The tone was more challenging now, and Nigel's rose to meet it. It wasn't a voice Louise had ever heard him use before.

'No. Please leave the premises.'

'You a fucking racist?'

'I'm calling the police. '

As Nigel went to close the door, Holly jammed the rubber-tipped end of her crutch in the jamb. 'He's not done nothing!'

Jigging with impatience, the man whipped his phone from the pocket of his jeans.

'You want to see the kind of slag she is?'

'I'm a lawyer. I'm sure the police would be delighted to see it and treat it as evidence.'

'Fuck you, man!'

'Nish—I haven't got nothing to do with him!'

Holly was squirming her way past Nigel, but he managed to grab her by the elbows and hang on in spite of her hysterical, twisting anguish. Louise forced herself forward.

'What happened to the police?'

This was Patrick, still uncomprehending as Nigel wrenched writhing Holly back. She was screaming—'Fuck *off*! I fucking love him!'—trying to wriggle out of Nigel's grasp, but then with a scream of pain she lost balance and fell, dropping the crutch. As Nigel lurched to help her, Holly's so-called boyfriend started forward. Before he could come in through the unprotected entrance, Patrick stepped up and slammed the heavy door with a violence that shuddered the elderly frame. The man's shouts, muted by the shut door, rose into a squawk of alarm, immediately echoed by Patrick on their side. Louise saw why: the vibration from the frame appeared, in an extraordinary accumulation, to be spreading, so that as she watched, the plaster above the door heaved and, with an uncanny groan from deep in the wall, a crack thunderbolted from the top of the door frame up into the ceiling. For a slow-motion moment, they all gaped as a much larger movement overtook the front of the house. The wall buckled.

'Louise!'

Nigel. To the monumental percussion of tumbling masonry, he had dragged hold of Holly and was staggering back with her towards the kitchen. Louise tried to bundle Patrick after them, but he thrashed her away, yelping. Blinding dust rose. She needed to get Jamie.

'Just get into the garden, away from the house! Look after Holly!' As Nigel shouted, pushing the whimpering girl at her, Louise realised she herself was screaming.

She took Holly as Nigel headed back towards the stairs, squinting and coughing through a fog of plaster dust. Louise expected everything to collapse beneath him, but there was no further catastrophe as he made it to the top. She shifted herself.

'Patrick, come on.'

This time, he followed her, out through the kitchen. As she, sobbing Holly and Patrick made their way into the garden, Louise saw that the back of the building was still undamaged. Outside, the noise had already subsided from the first cacophony of the main disaster into the individual smashing of bricks from the front of the house as they fell. The wall had collapsed outwards. Taking no risks, she led the three of them to the sea end, as far away from the house as possible. The rain still poured down, a small shock with everything else that was going on. More bricks fell. She wondered if the man who had come for Holly was lying crushed beneath the sundered porch. It would serve the bastard right.

She cried out in relief as Nigel shepherded Jamie into the garden to join them. Jamie only had his boxers on; he'd been in bed, slept through the whole thing. Suddenly, as she hung on to him, Louise wanted to laugh. She must be hysterical herself. Nigel sat down heavily on the soaked grass as he fished for his phone. When he attempted to ring 999 his hands were trembling so badly that his fingers kept botching the keypad. As he finally got through, a new noise exploded out at the front of the house. They all flinched, then relaxed as they recognised its normality: a car engine. Holly's boyfriend had survived, then, and in a state fit to drive. At this, even Holly stopped screaming.

'What's the address again?' Nigel asked Patrick, as the operator waited. Patrick looked past him at the house, too stunned to answer.

As Jamie pulled the phone away from his uncle, Louise put a hand on Nigel's shoulder. Beyond hysteria, a brimming excitement animated her as she took in the disaster they had all survived.

'Nidge, love,' she said, squeezing, 'It's all all right. She knows what she's doing. Mum.'

Nigel slumped his head on his knees. The sound that came out of him was the only dry thing around them.

While they waited for the emergency services—all of them, they'd been promised—Nigel remained on the lawn. He'd rung Sophie to fetch him. Louise had Holly leaning into her, stroking her hair to comfort her, like she'd done ever since she was tiny, as Holly took long, shivering breaths. Patrick sat, a little way away, on the stone bench near the sundial. The rain ran down his flattened hair, dripping off his face. Jamie veered ever closer to the house, despite Louise's warnings, trying to get a proper look.

'What was it you wanted to tell me?' Louise asked Nigel, remembering. 'About what Mum did?'

'What?'

'Before it all kicked off,' she prompted. 'You were saying, about something she did.'

Nigel rubbed the bottom of his nose with a pointed forefinger, the way he'd always done when she put him on the spot. Nidge. Those unmarked, schoolboy hands.

'She made me choose.' Nigel faced up into the sky that spilled endlessly down on them. They might not need the fire brigade, Louise thought. Surely nothing could catch fire in this.

'When she left Dad. She said there wasn't enough money for Patrick to send both of us to school, so I could choose. You could go, or me, or neither of us. She said it was up to me. We could stick together if we wanted, but it was up to me.'

Holly raised her head. 'What a shitty thing to do. What she do that for?'

Behind them, Patrick made a noise as the sirens came to rescue them.

'I never knew that,' said Louise.

After

NIGEL HAD probably been rude to the neighbour, but it was clear to him she'd only turned up to gawp. Sophie, God knows how, remembered her name was Jenny, and was far more polite, despite trying to wrangle the boys into the car at the same time as rationalising all the crap they were attempting to cram in the boot. The woman sat astride her bike, undeterred by his offhandedness.

'Oh dear,' she said, staring at the scaffolding that buttressed the wreckage of the house's façade. Black and yellow danger tape was draped from it at intervals, fluttering against the weather, which had reverted to some sort of seasonal normality. The police, deranged with health and safety, had only agreed to let them back in the house the previous day. Louise was in there now with her son, foraging for clothes after a week of camping at their B and B.

'Still, I suppose that's why we have insurance . . .'

Sophie and Nigel shared a look. In fact, because Patrick had bought the house for cash, with the heady profit of *Bloody Empire*'s monetisation, it seemed there had been no obligation on Patrick and Sara to take out buildings insurance. Patrick was predictably hazy when Nigel questioned him, and in any case, Nigel suspected that the failure to carry out any sort of maintenance would render any miraculously underwritten claim invalid. Patrick had already announced himself content to let the injured structure crumble. Whether it was the house or Mia's departure that had enfeebled him, he was suddenly very old. There would have to be serious conversations about his future.

Jenny, twisting to plunder the retro spotted panniers that balanced across her bike, produced a cling-filmed casserole dish, kept carefully horizontal.

'I thought you might be able to use this. Don't worry about the dish, it's an old one.'

Sophie accepted the contribution, slightly at a loss. They were, finally, about to drive back to Surrey. 'How kind. I'm sure Nigel's sister . . .'

She placed the gift on the top of the car. 'I'm sorry we can't ask you in. We're not allowed, actually, it isn't safe—'

'Diurnal shift.' This was Olly, who greatly enjoyed the phrase pronounced by the structural engineer who had driven up from St Ives.

'The weather,' Nigel explained. 'It was really wet, then really dry, then wet. Everything moved.'

And, the engineer had added, the house should have been underpinned years ago; all those cracks and dodgy door and window frames were a sign.

'Absolutely . . .' Jenny shook her head, sympathetically incapacitated by negatives. 'And you'd just had work done, hadn't you?'

Taking sledgehammers to walls hadn't helped, said the engineer. Good old Mia.

'So I'm afraid . . .' Nigel waved his hand at the house, aiming for dismissal.

'Of course. I was just on my way to Crantock.'

The woman wriggled something else from her pannier and offered it to him: a clear blue plastic file with some kind of thin document inside. What she said about it struggled to gain purchase in Nigel's understanding. His mother and Jenny had taken a class together in a neighbouring village a few years ago: creative writing. They'd all produced a pamphlet to mark their achievement at the end of the course: 'some pieces of life writing', Jenny called it. She'd come across it when she was tidying her desk and thought that it was something that Patrick—'or Sara's family', she amended—would want to have.

'Did Patrick know?'

Jenny shook her head, her grimace acknowledging what an incendiary pursuit it would have been for his mother to confess. Patrick had been approached to teach on sundry creative writing courses over the years. He'd always relished reporting his extravagant denunciations of these offers to collude in what he called 'the travesty of writing as industrial process'.

Just another of Sara's secrets then. Nigel took the folder. Finally finding his manners, he apologised for not offering so much as a cup of tea in return.

'Not to worry.' Jenny pushed off with one toned leg and, with a brief clumsiness, mounted the pedals. He and Sophie watched her cycle fluidly out of the drive. 'Take care!'

'Aren't you going to read it?' Sophie asked, as Nigel surmounted the casserole dish with the file.

He shrugged. A fugitive thought. Less a memory than a leftover feeling attached to a memory. *Bloody Empire*, the famous visit, when he'd been ferried from school for the opening night of the West End transfer. Seventeen, the quinine bitterness of the interval gin and tonic, arousal from the very idea of those breasts bared on the stage minutes before, the involvement in his own randiness of Patrick and his mother and the familiar rutting heat between them. Standing at the bar, a sudden interruption to that, an unseen barrier. It came from his mother, dazzling in the kind of dress no one wore any more. The feeling she emanated was distinct from the mood of the *Bloody Empire* audience, although just as connected to what they'd all seen on stage.

'How you can say that's me, I don't know.'

Is that what she'd said? Something like it: ironic, throwaway, the teasing flatness she used for intimacy. But in that small moment as she'd handed Patrick her cigarette packet, just before Patrick had landed the cigarette and bowed to take the light she offered, he quailed in a way Nigel had never seen, before or since. He had looked lost, frightened even. Why?

Nigel struggled after the memory. Surely she must have been proud, as well as a bit baffled, as everyone was. Shocked, perhaps, as well. There had been a current of indulgent pleasure among the interval audience in exercising their outrage. He remembered stumped eye rolls and half-sentences ('Well!', 'Strong stuff!') and rueful puffings, none of them from Mum. That wouldn't have been her style, which was always opaque. 'Serene' was the traditional interpretation, although considering it now, that mask-like attendance on other people's emotions, Nigel wondered. Had she been thinking, let alone feeling, anything at all?

'They meant the world to each other.' That's what Louise always said. For-thine-is-the-kingdom-the-power-and-the-glory-for-ever-and-ever-amen.

He took the dish and file from the top of the car.

'I'm just popping inside.'

Plaster dust obscured the details of every surface, with Louise's and Jamie's footprints stark on the stairs. Sneezing, he followed their trail. They were on the landing, hauling a bin liner stuffed with bedding between them. Nigel saw the blurred tattoo rose on Louise's forearm, its stem and petals faded with age, all its colours reverting to blue. He always forgot about it, surprised each time by the sight. Imagine, his little sister with that on her arm.

'It's all right, we can manage,' she told him, the catch in her breath worse from the effort. But she looked pleased to see him.

Nigel conjured his mother. A warm, scented shape; the lively metallic curls of her hair that he loved to wind around his fingers; a silent figure, careful with her spoon at breakfast; her back, dressed for work or dressing-gowned, going out of the door of whichever room he and Louise were noisily inhabiting, playing one of their favourite games. Warm, warmer, boiling hot, colder . . . *How you can say that's me, I don't know.*

Nigel hoisted the casserole, the file balanced on its lid.

'I've got something for you,' he said.

The young woman wears a short blue mac that barely covers the top of her long slim legs. Her knees and ankles show every bone. Even with tights on they look polished. It's hard for her to find tights to fit, her legs are so long, but stockings are impossible with short skirts. At the weekends she wears jeans but during the week she has to look smart for work.

The young woman works at a chemist's called Wilkinsons. The couple who run it aren't called Wilkinson, they bought the business off them. The couple are called Mr and Mrs Monette. They came from down south somewhere, although Mr Monette is Scottish. They seem old to the girl but they are probably in their fifties. They are both quiet people and good to work for. Mr Monette is the pharmacist and Mrs Monette works behind the till. Although he doesn't talk much, Mr Monette has a noise he makes when he's working in the back room where he makes up the prescriptions. It sounds like he's trying to spit something out of his mouth using the tip of his tongue, something fiddly like the pith of an orange, although there isn't anything there. He was shell-shocked during the war when he was a teenager. The other thing about Mr Monette is that he has one very long fingernail. It is on the little finger of his left hand. It is much longer than any of his other nails and always very clean and filed into a point. The girl doesn't know if it has some use in Mr Monette's work as a pharmacist, but every time she sees the nail it surprises her. Mrs Monette has nothing unusual about her. She eats two Ryvita for her dinner every day that she takes out of a pale blue Tupperware box with a lid coloured like an old toenail. She also has a tomato in the box that she dips into a twist of salt along with a hardboiled egg. After her food she smokes one Embassy Regal. It's the only cigarette she has all day. She keeps herself smart and has her hair set every week. Her hair is dyed jet black. The Monettes don't have any children.

The young woman has two children. She has worked at the chemists since they started at school and the boy was old enough to have a key to let them both in after. They watch TV until she gets back to make them their tea. Their dad usually gets in from work as she's putting it on the plates. She had the boy when she was seventeen and the girl when she was twenty, so she is still young. Sometimes she feels young and sometimes she thinks thirty is ancient and her life is over. There are a lot of old people who come to the chemists and they all tell her that she's young. They call her a lovely young lass, 'a lovely young lass like you', they say. They all take tablets or have trusses or some of the old ladies have feet and legs that swell out of normal shoes so that they have to wear slippers and can barely walk. They take tablets for it, it's called elephantiasis but the tablets don't make much difference. She feels sorry for them, but she doesn't want to be that old. Sometimes, the way she gets whistled at or talked to she hates it, but usually it's nice, like her legs and all the rest are a present she's been given. If you were given a watch, a really expensive one, no one would expect you to keep it in the box. They'd say it was meant to tell the time.

It's not all old people who come to the chemist's. There are mothers with babies and children, especially in the mornings. There's a big scale for weighing babies in the front of the shop and it's something for the mothers to do. She helps, because Mrs Monette is nervous of babies, who wriggle around in the slippy enamel bowl of the scale like fish and often cry. There is a box of deep red glucose lollies with vitamin C kept near the till and mothers buy these for their older children for behaving while their little brothers and sisters get weighed. Her own daughter always begs for a lolly when she comes into the shop and the girl gives her one. She puts the money in the till for it as well, a couple of coppers, and Mrs Monette never stops her, never says it's on the house. That's what she's like.

Lads come in for johnnies, teenage lads on a bet, some with their mates, and Mrs Monette serves them so that sometimes they end up buying one of the lollies or a packet of Victory Vs instead and scarpering. Older men don't come in for johnnies. They must get them somewhere else. Mr Monette fills prescriptions for the pill, and the girl gets her own prescription filled there. The pill makes her feel heavy and headachy, although it's worth it not to have another baby. The pills come in a pale pink dial, turned for each day of the week. The chemist is so old-fashioned, full of polished wood, and pink plastic seems odd in it, but the pills arrive in boxes and they must dispense going on for a hundred a month to married women like her, or women who say they're married. It's the modern world.

If she thinks about it now, the chemist is more a place for women than men. Old men come in, but only if their wives are dead and can't collect their medicine for them. Then there are the babies, the ways of avoiding having babies, the pads and belts and tampons, the teats and gripe water and teething pegs and rusks, the jars of Cow & Gate, the pile cream and the rose water and the pots of Nivea and Atrixo, the boxes of fudge and biscuits you are meant to eat instead of food to help you slim, the Complan and Lucozade to build you up when you're too ill to eat. He doesn't want any of this when he comes into the shop. If you were making him up you'd think he wanted johnnies, and he wouldn't take Victory Vs instead. But he's lost.

There's a taxi outside and it doesn't know where to take him. She doesn't know anyone who takes taxis, unless they're coming back from the airport on holiday.

'I'm looking for the college,' he says. 'I'm giving a talk.'

His voice is deep, with a stranger's accent. He's left the door open and brought the frosty draught in with him. He probably swears. He's wearing a jacket that doesn't matter and his hair is greasy black and beautiful. His eyes aren't as dark as his hair, but they are beautiful too, like an animal's eyes, so alive, so outside her and everything about her. Him. She can't believe the sight of him, but there he is.

Falling in love is like a song on the radio.

ACKNOWLEDGEMENTS

WARMEST THANKS GO to Jill Bialosky and all at Norton for supportive editing, and to my US agent Zoe Pagnamenta. A huge thank-you to Anna Webber, who engaged with the book at an early stage and provided invaluable comments and encouragement. And to Ursula Doyle at Virago, without whom it would be a very different book—and not in a good way. To Clara Glynn and John Archer for first-draft Drymen dinners and company; Clare and Brian Linden for generous use of the Retreat, which made all the difference; and Deborah Dooley and Bob (www.retreatsforyou.co.uk), for Sheepwash hospitality at another crucial point. Meike Ziervogel, for Louise Bourgeois. Kate Lock, the most constant and generous friend any woman could have. Gus and Julia, for being such good company: no offence taken. And to my husband, Andrew Clifford, who makes everything possible in all ways.